Partners in Crime
By
Cheryl Russell

Chapter One

Justin knocked on the door. Silence. Finding the door ajar he walked in. "Mr Matthews," he called. No response. The flat was eerily quiet which was odd as he was expected. He was due to do a flat inspection.

He walked around the flat anyway. Reaching the bathroom, he opened the door with some reluctance but couldn't have said why. He peered around the door and hurriedly left the flat with a scream. The bath was ketchup red.

Ellie, living next door, heard the noise and left her flat to investigate. She didn't see Justin leaving as he'd been in a rush. Seeing the open door she entered. She could find nothing suspicious, although why she should assume it was something dodgy she didn't know. On entering the bathroom she was horrified at what she saw. Had there been an accident? There were no signs of blood elsewhere. Maybe they had got themselves to hospital.

She didn't really know her neighbours. She couldn't even say how many people lived there. She smiled in passing but rarely a word was exchanged. It was different from decades ago which her mother used to speak so fondly of when everyone knew everyone and helped out if necessary. There had been a real sense of community back then which had sadly gone.

Ellie went back to her flat and picked up her mobile to call the police. Within minutes they had arrived. Ellie, looking out for them, met them at the door and told them what she had seen.

One officer stayed outside to speak to Ellie whilst the other one entered the flat, heading straight for the bathroom.

"Hello, I'm PC Nally and you are?"

"Ellie."

"Ok Ellie, you look as if you've had a bit of a shock. Maybe we should go inside and sit down."

Ellie nodded and allowed the officer to lead the way back into her flat.

"Right can you tell me everything you know."

"That's not much. I heard a scream and footsteps running away. I went along to see if someone needed help and found the bath full of blood. It was then I came back to call you."

PC Nally nodded. "Do you know who lived there?"

"Sorry no. There is definitely a male but I don't have a name for him. Sometimes I can hear a female voice as well but never met a woman."

PC Nally looked up as his colleague entered.

"Ellie this is PC Dander."

"Hello," said Ellie.

"Can I have a word for a second, outside," said PC Dander.

PC Nally stood up and left Ellie alone.

"Does she know anything?" asked Dander.

Nally shook his head.

"Hmm, we have an interesting situation here. We have no person wounded, dead or alive but what appears to be a bath with blood in it. I've had a quick look around the flat and found a knife with a serrated edge with what looks like traces of blood."

"Should we get forensics here?"

"Yes. It would help if we had a name for the occupant of the flat and as much as we can know about them."

"Ellie doesn't know anything, or so she says. She doesn't have a name except that it's a male resident. Occasionally she'll hear a female voice but hasn't met her."

"Not helpful."

"You wait for forensics and I'll speak to Ellie. I can't believe she doesn't know anything about her neighbour."

Dander went into see Ellie. Sitting down beside her without being invited he spoke, "Hello Ellie, I know you've had a bit of a shock but I need to know everything you can tell me about the person living there."

Ellie shook her head. "I can't help you. All I know is there is a male who lives alone but he has a girlfriend who visits regularly."

"How do you know it's a girlfriend."

Ellie shrugged. "I just assumed it must be."

"In my job you don't assume, you get hard facts."

"But I'm not in your job."

"What is it you do?"

"I'm a podiatrist."

Dander nodded, not really interested but thought it might be a way into getting information out of Ellie. He was sure she must know more than she was letting on.

"Can you give us a name?"

Ellie shook her head. "We never exchanged names."

"I'm finding it hard to believe you know absolutely nothing about your neighbour."

"We only exchange pleasantries, hello, how are you, that sort of thing."

Dander nodded. He stood up to leave saying, "We'll probably want to speak to you again, so make yourself available."

"I can't give you anymore information than you already have."

"You'd be surprised what you can remember if you have to."

On her own again, Ellie found herself shivering. It was the shock she knew.

Picking up her phone she found the name she wanted and made a call.

"Hi Lucy."

"Hi, are you all right?"

"Not really. You won't believe what's just happening. I discovered the bath full of blood in my neighbours flat."

"What? How come you were in his flat?"

Ellie briefly went through all that had happened.

"And there was no blood anywhere else and no body?"

"No."

"How strange. With that much blood you would expect to find someone probably in the bath. They can't have got far if they left of their own volition."

"I know. It's all very odd."

"Are you sure it's blood and not hair dye."

"But he's male. Men don't usually dye their hair."

"True."

"But what about his girlfriend?"

"I hadn't thought of that. Oh dear I hope I haven't called the police for nothing."

"I was thinking, I hope you have. It's awful to think of someone having lost their life. What about the scream you heard that led you to investigate? Could that have been the victim?"

"I don't think so as I then heard footsteps hurrying away. If that was the victim they wouldn't have been able to rush like that."

"You've got a point there. Also if that person was the perpetrator they wouldn't have been able to rush if they were carrying the body."

"Why would they have to be carrying a body?"

"The body wasn't in the flat so must be somewhere else, which means they must have been moved by someone."

"My brains addled."

"I'm not surprised. I would come round but with all this snow we've had overnight I can't move the car."

"That's all right. We should get together soon and discuss it."

"Are you opening our detective agency again?" asked Lucy.

"Yes, I think I am."

"Goody. That will bring some interest into our mundane lives. Better than ingrowing toenails anyway."

"That's what I thought."

Ellie and Lucy were best friends. The previous year they had solved the death of their supervisor with some help from Lucy's husband, Mick. The police had been nowhere near solving it. They had done it with the help of footprints which of course was their thing, both being podiatrists and working at the local hospital. The murderer had been a colleague of theirs.

....

PCs Nally and Dander were standing just outside the flat while forensics gave the flat a thorough going over.

"Ok," said one to the officers. "We're taking a sample of the blood to analyse and the knife away to see if it matches. We need to know if it is actually blood we are dealing with. It could be completely innocent though, just an accident and the supposed victim now in A & E being stitched up."

"That's a thought. We should see what we can find out."

"Now you need us forensic guys to tell you your job."

"Sarcasm will get you nowhere."

"It's nice to get the better of you occasionally."

"We have to work together."

"I know."

"Well, we'll be off now to see what we can find out at the hospital."

"Bye. We'll let you know as soon as we have some answers."

Dander nodded before walking out, leaving Nally to follow behind.

Chapter Two

Ellie was looking out of the window thinking how beautiful the snow looked. What made it more perfect was the unexpected day off work it gave her. It was sunny now which added to the beauty as it sparkled on the recent snow. The sky looked as if there was a load more to follow but for the moment there was enough on the ground. Across the road Ellie could see a mother and son building a snowman in their front garden. They looked as if they were having fun. How Ellie would have loved to be doing that, but she hadn't been blessed with children. She now lived alone but not by choice. Her husband was in prison, serving time for a vicious assault on her body which had come out of the blue. She hadn't experienced anything like it in all the years they had been married and then suddenly he'd turned on her. She had always thought him gentle, mild mannered until that point. If she allowed herself to think about it she didn't understand what had changed him. For a few months she had lived with Mick and Lucy until she had got to the point of needing her own space again. She was now renting this flat in the short term although hoped to be able to buy her own place soon. Renting had so many disadvantages which she struggled with.

Ellie shook her head, bringing her back to the present. She didn't like to think of the past year and all that had happened. She continued looking out when her eyes were drawn to the footprints going to and from the main door into the flats. Putting her shoes and coat on and grabbing her ipad she rushed downstairs and stood just outside the door. Going into the camera app she started photographing the footprints. She didn't know why but realised this might give them a way forward in this latest mystery that needed solving. She was wondering which prints went in which direction. Realising she needed a tape measure to know the length of the prints she hurried back inside. She gave a little shiver as she did so. It was freezing cold outside as could be expected in such snowy conditions.

She took as many measurements as possible although it was difficult with so many different prints out there.

Going back inside she sat down to properly analyse them. How many different prints were there? She couldn't be sure. In fact she couldn't properly tell which direction they were going in as many merged into one enormous print. Unless they had a monster making them and she was certain that wasn't the case. This was real life not some sort of science fiction fantasy thing, the Lochness monster it was not!

"Hi Lucy."

"Ellie, don't tell me you've solved the mystery without me."

"No it's not that. I've just taken photos of the footprints in the snow."

"You mean you think they will be the answer like our last case?"

"Well, maybe, oh I don't know what I'm thinking."

"What was the reason for the call?"

"I wanted a second opinion really."

"Hmm that's a bit difficult when I can't see the photos or the actual prints. There is definitely no way I can get anywhere today, sorry it will have to wait."

"I know. I don't know what it is I wanted really. I wouldn't want you to come out in this. It looks like an ice rink out there."

"It is I can assure you of that. I tried to go to tescos but abandoned the effort before I reached the end of the drive."

"Look why don't I email you the prints I have. Maybe I can get in next door to take photos of the bath and of the whole flat as well."

"That sounds a good idea. It will give me something to do instead of sitting here twiddling my thumbs and getting bored."

Disconnecting the call, Ellie got on with the business of sending attachments in her email for Lucy to look at.

………

"What did Ellie want?" asked Mick, Lucy's husband.

"You know that bath with blood in it that I told you about earlier, well now she's taken photos of footprints in the snow going backwards and forwards. She's going to email them to me as she wants my opinion."

"Uh oh. I sense the detective duo will be open for business again soon. Didn't you get enough of that with the Phyllis affair last year."

"It seems not, besides it gives us something to focus on to give our brains some work. It's good to use our brains occasionally."

"You mean you have a brain?"

Lucy got up and went over to where he was relaxing in the armchair and swotted him with the book she had been reading until Ellie phoned.

"I suppose I asked for that," said Mick giving a bit of a laugh.

"You certainly did. We have one brain cell between the two of us I'll have you know."

"That's always helpful. I always knew you two couldn't function without the other."

"You know us too well."

"I certainly should do. How long have we been married? Twenty five years and you two were joined at the hip even then."

"Very true. Ah that sounds like an email coming through. I'd better check that, it's probably from Ellie."

Sure enough when Lucy switched her ipad on she received the email plus attachments from Ellie.

"I can't believe it. Mick, listen to this. "Next doors flat was shut up but I used my bank card to open it. Don't ask me how I did it. I picked it up from watching a detective programme a while back. I always knew it would come in handy." She'll get us both in trouble one day, I'm sure of it."

"I agree. What possessed her to break in? Not only that but it's a crime scene, well we assume it is anyway."

"I know. I really can't imagine what she'll come up with next. I think I'll have to disown her at this point."

"Don't do that. You are the sensible one of the two of you. She needs you to keep her out of real trouble."

"I agree on that point. I'm not sure she listens to me though. I just follow along with her and hope for the best."

"Anyway, come on let's have a look at these photos. You might as well use me as a sounding board while I'm here. I could see something you're both missing."

"Of course I'll include you. It's more like the detective triplet not the duo you suggested. If it wasn't for you we would never have worked out who killed Phyllis and we would have been killed as well."

Mick got up and went to sit on the sofa besides his wife. With the ipad between them they studied the photos that Ellie had sent across.

"Hmm," said Mick. "I'm not sure what you'll get out of the footprints as they merge into one as I'm sure Ellie noticed. There are also what look like bird prints as well just to confuse the issue."

"Do you think it's possible to work out if they're male or female? It might narrow things down a bit."

"I suppose you could measure the prints. If Ellie can get outside to do it safely that is. Also, what neither of you seem to have thought of is that the police were going in and out which will confuse the issue. I really don't see what you hope to achieve with the footprints."

Lucy looked downcast. "I'll phone her and see what she says."

A few minutes later she put the phone down and turned to Mick. "She says she'll give it a try."

....

Ellie wrapped up warm with hat, gloves and scarf and out she went. She also had her fleece lined boots as well so her feet wouldn't get cold, or not any colder than they already were anyway. Crouching down she fiddled with the tape measure finding it difficult to do anything accurately with her gloves on. She had no intention of taking them off though. She wasn't that stupid.

"What are you doing?" called a voice from a downstairs window.

"Oh hello," said Ellie looking up from what she was doing.

"I'm Tammy by the way."

"I'm Ellie."

"Nice to meet you. You haven't been living here long have you?" asked Tammy.

"No. I only moved in three months ago."

"What exactly are you doing? I was watching you and becoming intrigued had to ask."

"Did you hear all the commotion earlier. Someone screamed and ran off. I went and discovered blood in the bath of my next door neighbour."

Tammy gasped. "You mean Ashley? I think he lives there anyway. Is he all right?"

"If that's his name then yes it's him. I don't know if he's ok. The flat was empty. I called the police because I thought it was suspicious looking by the amount of blood there."

"I didn't hear anything. I must have slept through it. I'm not well you see."

"I'm sorry to hear that. Can I do anything?" asked Ellie.

"No. There's nothing anyone can do."

"Can I ask what the problem is?"

"ME," said Tammy.

"Oh no, I'm sorry to hear that. From everything I've read about it, it sounds a nasty illness."

"It is. I wouldn't wish it on my worst enemy. I rarely get out of the house."

"Oh no that sounds boring."

"Not really. I feel too ill to be bored. I have to spend most of the day resting."

"Well look if you need anything just let me know. I'll put my phone number under your door so you only have to give me a call. I work full time but should be able to help at other times."

"Thank you. I appreciate that."

Tammy shut her window and disappeared inside, needing a lay down as the conversation and standing at the window and tired her out.

Ellie looked after her thoughtfully. She had noticed how Tammy went pale at hearing about Ashley. There was more going on there than it first appeared. She would make sure she had another chat at some point. At the very least she would find out more about who Ashley was. It seemed that Tammy knew him personally and not just as a neighbour to say hello to in passing. Very interesting. She would find a reason to knock on her door over the next couple of days. Not straightaway as she might be too tired to talk and then it would achieve nothing.

Ellie crouched back down going back to the job she had been doing until Tammy had interrupted. This time she managed to finish the job and hurried back inside wanting to get warm quickly. It really was bitterly cold and if she wasn't mistaken the sky looked full of more snow.

Quickly she sent another email to Lucy with details of measurements and also the conversation she'd had with Tammy and her suspicions.

Chapter Three

The sun shone brightly on the snow making it look like beautiful diamonds.

"The snow does look lovely," said Lucy, when they were on their way to work.

"It certainly does. It causes such chaos though. I was starting to go stir crazy stuck in with nothing to do."

"I thought you would have solved our new mystery single handed by now."

"I'm not that clever you know. I rely on you as well."

"That's what I said to Mick. That we have one brain cell between us and need each other to function."

Ellie laughed. "You've got that exactly right. Oh it is good to get out of the house."

"You made that statement just now. Has the snow addled your brain or something that's making you repeat yourself."

Ellie glanced at her friend with a look on her face that didn't bode well. "If you weren't driving I would thump you."

"I'm glad I'm behind the wheel is all I can say," said Lucy pretending to be frightened as she gave an exaggerated shiver.

"It's been a whole week without work."

"I know. That means we'll be extra busy today. Oh well, nothing we can do about it. It is winter after all. I just wish we could go back to being children and enjoy ourselves playing in the snow. I could murder a good snow fight."

"I wouldn't use that word if I were you. Or a second body will turn up."

"A second body? What about the first one. To my knowledge there isn't a single one to start with."

"You're right. I'm just making assumptions as Ashley hasn't appeared again."

"Well, you're coming back to mine tonight and we can look at what we've got so far. The three of us will crack this so don't you worry."

"Three? I thought there were only two of us."

"You're forgetting Mick. He's been getting quite into it as well you know."

"Even better if we have Mick to help. Without him we would never have solved the first one."

"I know and he hasn't let me forget the last few days whenever I bring our latest adventure up in conversation."

Ellie laughed. "That sounds about right."

Arriving at work they hurried in and found everyone stood around gossiping.

"What's going on?" asked Lucy.

"We're just glad to be back. That snow was horrendous. I was getting bored at home," commented Paul.

"We were as well but guess what?"

"Sorry can't guess," said Chris.

"We are involving ourselves in another mystery," said Ellie before Lucy could speak.

"Just don't put it down to the wrong person this time," said Chris, with a note of bitterness in his voice.

Chris had been wrongly accused of the murder of Phyllis and had spent days in prison as a result of the two women's investigation so had every reason to be dubious about the friends involvement.

"Don't worry. My Mick will be helping us from the start this time."

"Wasn't he involved last time?" asked Paul, a note of scepticism in his voice.

"Yes but he left it to us until the end."

"Come on you lot get ready for the day," said Olivia the supervisor entering to see them all standing chatting.

The group disbursed and went about their business.

Lucy and Ellie didn't have a chance to get together until they were on their way home. They had a lot of paperwork to get through so had worked throughout their lunchbreak, eating sandwiches as they did so.

"Phew, am I glad today's over," said Ellie, sinking into the sofa, when they reached Lucy's house.

"No slacking. You can make us a cup of tea while I make a start on dinner."

"Do I have to?" grumbled Ellie. "I'm aching all over. I'm getting too old for this every day."

"If you are then so am I as we're both fifty. Come on get your lazy bottom off that sofa and come and help. I could murder a cuppa right now."

"You've got no sympathy. I don't know why I bother with you."

"You know where the door is," said Lucy.

"And miss out on your delicious shepherds pie no thanks," said Ellie, heaving herself up from the sofa and following Lucy to the kitchen.

"I knew it. Always thinking of your tummy you are."

"Not always, just this time every day. I'm always hungry after a long day at work as are you if only you'd admit to it."

"Ok if you insist."

"You two arguing again?" asked Mick entering the kitchen.

"I didn't hear you come in," said Lucy, stopping what she was doing and reaching up to her husband for a kiss.

"You wouldn't as you were having a go at each other as usual."

"You know us. Anyway we don't fall out seriously. It's just the way we are."

"You think I don't know that? I live here and witness it all the time. Even if you aren't together it will be over the phone or email."

"Very true," said Lucy, beginning to laugh.

"I've just put the kettle on if you want a coffee Mick," said Ellie.

"There's no if about it, you know I never say no to a coffee."

"Didn't think you would but thought I had better check."

"Are we eating and then getting down to business."

"You make it sound like work. It's been a long day the thought of work doesn't exactly thrill me," said Ellie.

"If you don't want to look at this latest mystery of yours we don't have to. I'm perfectly happy to just relax in front of the telly."

"Oh no you don't. You're helping us," said Lucy. "Well, that's in the oven, now we can relax over our drinks for a while before eating."

"Sounds good," said Ellie.

"Lazy bones," said Lucy, glancing affectionately at her friend.

"That's me always wanting the easy life."

"I don't know about that. You've involved yourself in another mystery that may or may not be another murder."

"I've convinced myself it already is a suspicious death."

"I know you have, even though you have no proof yet."

"You didn't see the bath. It was all bloody. Made me shiver it did."

"How can we investigate when we don't know the people involved? You didn't even see the person running away so we couldn't identify him if he reappeared," said Lucy.

Ellie shook her head looking downcast.

"Hey don't look like that. We'll find a way and I'm always up for a challenge."

The expression on Ellie's face lifted. "Thanks. I knew I could count on you. Anyway we know the lady downstairs now. We could find out what she knows about Ashley so there is a link there straight away."

"We don't know anything about his life though. Maybe he's a criminal and has upset the wrong people."

Ellie shivered and a brief look of fear crossed her face. "I don't want to get involved with some criminal gang."

"I'm sure it's nothing like that. You've never complained about the noise from him so I'm sure he is innocent of any wrongdoing."

"Let's hope so. I would be nice if his disappearance had a reasonable explanation."

"We are going to have to try and find out what the police have discovered to start with."

"They said they would want to speak to me again in case I remembered anything else. I'll have to mention Tammy to them and say she knows him and can identify him if necessary."

Mick nodded. He had been keeping quiet, just listening to the two women talk. He was a man of few words anyway but when these two got together it was a bit difficult to get a word in edgeways, not that he minded as he didn't. He was still in love with Lucy and was very fond of Ellie who spent as much time with them as she did in her own flat.

"This is all seems so hopeless," said Ellie.

"It doesn't have to be. Why don't you try and have a chat with Tammy and find out what you can about your neighbour. What sort of person is he for instance?" suggested Mick.

"Well I can try I suppose."

"It's not like you to be so negative, at least not at the beginning of an investigation," said Lucy.

"I think it's just that we don't know anything about him or his lifestyle."

"But we know someone who does so that's a way in."

"Ok, I'll try and speak to Tammy at the weekend."

"Great idea."

Chapter Four

"Hi, sorry I took so long to answer the door my legs are very painful today," said Tammy opening the door to find Ellie on the doorstep.

"That's ok, not a problem. Are you up for a chat. I thought I'd pop in to see how you were."

"Not really I'm not. Sorry. I was laying on the sofa dozing off."

"Well, how about I come in and make you a cup of tea," suggested Ellie.

"Hmm, ok."

Ellie, pleased to get over the threshold entered, having a good look around as she did so. She found herself in a pleasant living room. The black leather sofas fitted perfectly with the décor. There was a glass coffee table which sat on a lovely red rug. There were pictures up on the wall.

"Did you paint these yourself?"

Tammy nodded as she settled back on the sofa with her legs up so she was reclining. Ellie noticed the hot water bottle.

"They really are very good. Do you sell them?"

"No it's just my hobby."

"You should consider selling them. It would make you a bit of money."

"I can't remember the last time I painted anything. Certainly not in the two years I've been ill."

"That's a shame. Are you cold? I see you're using a hot water bottle."

"No, I use it to help with the pain. If you wouldn't mind refilling it though please it would be a big help."

"Of course I don't mind. I'm only too happy to help."

"Thank you. You see I'm on my own. My parents don't want to know and I lost most of my friends when I became ill."

"I'm sorry to hear that. That sounds really tough. Remember you've got me now. I'm only upstairs. I work full time but when I'm around I'm happy to help where I can. I have a close friend, Lucy, and I'm sure she would be as well."

"Thank you. I really appreciate it. I hate how these days people keep themselves to themselves. They don't even know who their neighbours are. Everyone leads such busy lives."

"Oh I know. Long gone are the days when there was a sense of community when everyone helped each other."

"Fortunately my arms are not affected so I can use the internet to order my shopping."

"That's lucky or I would have been happy to do yours when I do my own. Anyway I don't want to exhaust you standing here talking. Where's everything and I'll make the tea."

"Just look around in the kitchen. I usually leave the teabags out ready so it saves a bit of time. The less time I spend standing the better."

"How do you cook."

"I don't, I have ready meals that I can just stick in the microwave. I do have a carer coming in the mornings to help with a shower but that's it. Half an hour and she's gone."

"At least that's company for a short while."

"Is it? She never speaks, just says hello and at the end she mutters a hasty goodbye then she's out the door before I even respond."

"That doesn't sound good."

"It's better than being left on my own unable to shower properly."

"Can't you ask for a different carer?"

"Believe me she's the best of a bad lot. There are some who are quite rough and hurt my sensitive skin. Others won't even shower me properly they just want to get going to the next client. We're not people to them. In fact sometimes I think we're an inconvenience."

"That's awful. I had no idea it was like that. It must make you feel terrible."

Tammy shrugged. "You get used to it. The worst of it is, that if you try and say anything then it's you that's the problem not the carers. The managers get quite defensive. As for social services well, there response is worse."

"I don't know how you put up with it."

"I have no choice," said Tammy, who had been very matter of fact about it. She sounded to Ellie as if she was resigned to her lot in life which seemed so sad.

"Anyway I will get your tea now."

Ellie went through to the kitchen which was just as spotless and just so as the living room. Tammy might be ill but she kept her place spotless. She put her own small flat to shame and she wasn't ill so had no excuse."

Tea and hot water made and she carried them through to Tammy whose eyes were shut. Ellie set them down quietly and turned to make her way out not wanting to disturb Tammy.

"Thank you," whispered Tammy not opening her eyes.

"That's ok. You're welcome. I didn't mean to wake you."

"You didn't. I'm not asleep it's just easier sometimes to lay here with my eyes shut especially if I'm close to a migraine. Could I ask you a favour before you leave. Could you put the hot water bottle under my legs again."

"Of course I can."

Ellie went back to the sofa where she picked up the bottle and lifting Tammy's legs slightly slid the bottle under.

"Ahh," said Tammy, with pain etched across her face.

"Sorry, I didn't want to hurt you."

"It's ok everything hurts me today."

Ellie left on that note. She didn't know what she would say to Lucy as it wasn't right at all to ask Tammy about Ashley. It had upset her to see Tammy so obviously very ill and in a lot of pain. How could anyone go through so much and survive like that for years and years. It was no life at all.

After speaking to Tammy last time she had looked ME up and had been appalled at what she had discovered. She hadn't known people could die from it but she was sad to learn they did and for those who lived it could be like that for years with no change except for the worst. How could anyone live like that. It was a living death.

Ellie couldn't imagine what it must be like to suffer so terribly on your own. Not only that but it was compounded by disbelief from everyone around especially from professionals.

....

What happened with Tammy over the weekend?" asked Lucy as soon as Ellie got in the car prepared for work.

"Oh yeah, you know. Same old, same old."

"What's that supposed to mean?" asked Lucy.

"I didn't get far," said Ellie. "I left her after making a cup of tea and refilling her hot water bottom."

"Sounds really tough."

"It was. She did emphasise that it was a bad day for her and she isn't always that bad."

"I'm glad to hear it. Maybe you can persuade her to tell you all she knows."

"Don't hold your breath on that one. She is very controlled and very unwell. I feel quite sorry for her. There is one slightly odd thing though. She kept one door shut."

"So? What are you trying to say?" asked Mick.

"I dunno. It seems strange that's all. Every other door was open even the bathroom door. I just wonder what lies behind the closed door."

"Maybe she just wants to keep some privacy," suggested Lucy.

"You could be right."

"But you're not convinced," said Lucy.

Ellie shook her head. "There is something strange going on and I want to know what it is."

"Are you just being a nosy neighbour or are you suggesting she has something to hide. A dead body of Ashley in there maybe."

"No, I'm not saying that at all. Oh I don't know what I mean."

"Try again another day, but not too soon or she'll get suspicious. After all we're not the police but lowly podiatrists with private investigator as a side line."

"I'm glad you said as a side line as I was beginning to think you saw it as your main job. Firstly you solve the murder of Phyllis and now you have Ellie's neighbour disappearing. That is if he has. He could have been called away unexpectedly, have you even thought about that."

The two women looked shamefaced at Mick's comment. This hadn't occurred to them.

Ellie said after much thought, "That doesn't explain all the red in the bath."

"Very true," agreed Mick. "But it still stands, there could be a reasonable explanation."

"Well I should probably get going if I have to be up for work in the morning. See you tomorrow Lucy."

"Great see you then. Don't forget it's your turn to drive."

"I won't."

After Ellie had left Lucy moved next to Mick and snuggled up to him. "That's better," he said. "As much as I like Ellie she feels in the way sometimes and prevents us from cuddling."

"I know. I'm sure she wouldn't mind but I feel awkward after all that happened with Simon."

"Has the divorce come through yet."

"She hasn't heard anything. She chased it up last week with her solicitor and they said it was all in hand it's just taking time. The system it seems is very slow with so many other petitions for divorce. She just has to be patient."

"Does it make it slower with Simon being in prison?"

"I don't know."

"I'm sure you'll be the first to hear when anything does happen. At least we know he has agreed to it."

"He had no choice really after the way he attacked her like that. I still can't believe it happened though. He appeared so gentle and mild mannered and then he suddenly exploded and became a raging bull overnight."

Mick nodded and gave a yawn. "I'm going up I think. I feel extra tired tonight, although I don't know why."

"I'll just wash these cups up and then I'll be with you."

Mick went slowly up the stairs. He didn't know why but he felt exceptionally tired. His limbs started feeling heavy as he heaved one foot in front of the other.

Lucy hummed to herself as she washed up. Suddenly she heard a loud noise. She couldn't describe it but she almost dropped the cup she was holding and raced up the stairs. Her heart went cold as it sank. Her beloved Mick was on the floor.

"Mick can you hear me? Darling, I'm here. I'm just going to ring for an ambulance."

She fumbled with her phone and made the emergency call.

"Is he breathing?" asked the operator.

"Yes I think so," said Lucy putting her hand on his chest and felt the rhythmic rise and fall.

"An ambulance is on its way. Don't worry they'll be there in a few minutes."

Lucy nodded then realised the man on the other end of the phone couldn't see it.

The next instance she heard the doorbell went into its familiar tune. Lucy raced down the stairs so fast it was a miracle she didn't fall. It was with much relief that she opened the door to let in the two paramedics on the doorstep. They very quickly got to work assessing the still unconscious Mick. Lucy was in a panic, but tried to hide it, not wanting to take up their time when they needed to be with her wonderful husband.

"Is it ok if I ring my friend?" asked Lucy.

"Of course you can," said the paramedic who had introduced himself as Brian. "In fact it's a good idea if you do."

He didn't say anything but the look he and his colleague had shared was that Mick might not make it. They needed to do an ECG to confirm but they both felt he'd had a serious heart attack.

Lucy quickly got through to Ellie. As soon as Ellie spoke Lucy burst into tears.

Ellie very concerned for her friend asked, "What's happened?"

Lucy unable to speak, willingly passed the phone to Brian who held his hand out for it. "Hello, my name is Brian and I'm a paramedic attending the scene."

Ellie gasped, "What's happened?" she asked, only just able to get the words out as fear clutched her chest.

"Mick has had an episode and is currently……"

"Tell Lucy I'm on my way."

"It would be best if you meet us at the hospital as we'll be leaving in the next few minutes."

Ellie disconnected the call and rushed out to her car. She had only just got in when she got the news. She was close to tears but knew it wasn't the time for that. She needed to be there as her friend would need her to be strong. Whatever was wrong with Mick it didn't sound good.

………..

Lucy felt sick. The ambulance was racing to the hospital and all the bends in the roads at the speed they were going was setting off the old familiar travel sickness she'd had as a child. Fortunately she had grown out of it but now it had resurfaced.

"Are you all right?" asked Brian concerned at the strange pallor on her face.

Lucy shook her head, unable to answer, as if she did the vomit would come up.

Brian, through his twenty year experience, saw what was happening and passed her a bowl, only just in time.

When she felt a bit better she managed to get the words out, "Travel….sickness…"

Brian nodded. "I understand but we need to go at speed. Your husband is seriously ill. We can't be certain as the ECG was inconclusive but it's possible he's had a heart attack."

Lucy let out a scream. "Not my Mick," she cried, desperation in her voice.

"Try not to worry," said Brian taking her hand. "He'll be in the best place. They'll see him straight away and assess him. You'll know more then."

Lucy nodded. She looked across at her husband laying quiet and still on the trolley, hooked up to machines so they could monitor him on the journey. Where had her active husband gone. She'd never known him be so still. He was never ill. He was always in robust health. She was terrified of losing him. How would she cope? She couldn't remember a time when she was single and living alone.

"Ok we're almost here now," said Brian. "If you get out first then we can get Mick out."

Lucy stood up but her legs turned to jelly. She managed to climb down from the ambulance and waited for them to get Mick out. She followed them into A & E. They rushed Mick into the resuscitation unit but wouldn't let Lucy in. She was led to the relatives room to await news. She hadn't been there long when the door opened and Ellie entered. Lucy stood up and went into Ellie's waiting arms, tears flowing freely.

"What happened?" asked Ellie when Lucy had calmed down a bit.

"I'm not sure. He was on his way to bed and I was going to follow him after washing up. I heard a strange sound and went running up the stairs to find Mick had collapsed at the top. They think he's had a heart attack."

"Oh no. I'm so sorry. What are the doctors saying?"

"They haven't said anything. I haven't seen a doctor since we got here. I got sent here while they assess him. It's the waiting that's awful."

"I'm here now. I won't leave you until we know what's happening. You're not on your own."

"But you have to go to work tomorrow. You need sleep."

"Work can do without us for once. I'm not leaving you like this. Besides, I won't sleep not knowing what is going on here."

Lucy nodded. She didn't pursue the conversation further for she was glad that Ellie was staying with her. She didn't feel strong enough to face whatever was happening on her own.

It seemed like forever to Lucy but was in fact less than half an hour before the door opened to admit a doctor. Lucy stood up.

"Sit down please," he said in a lovely deep, baritone voice. "My name is Dr Patch. Your husband has had a heart attack. It's quite a severe one. When he was brought in it was touch and go for a while. He's stable now and will be taken in intensive care as soon as a bed becomes available."

Lucy was stunned into silence. Ellie seeing this asked, "Will he be ok?"

"I can't say anything for certain at the moment. He's in a bad way. It will be a long recovery, if he makes it that far."

"Is he going to die?" asked Lucy, eventually finding her voice.

"I can't say anything at the moment. I'm sorry. We'll know more in the next day or two."

"I can't lose him."

"We're doing everything we can."

"Can I see him?"

"Yes, but just a few minutes. He's unconscious still. I must warn you he's hooked up to machines at the moment which can look scary."

Ellie and Lucy followed the doctor out of the room and down a long corridor to where Mick was laying. Lucy rushed up to him and would have flung herself onto him had she not been held back by a nurse.

"Be careful. We don't want these leads coming out."

Lucy held on to Ellie's hand so tight that Ellie was hard pressed not to gasp.

"We'll be taking him up to ICU shortly. The best thing you can do now is to go home and get some sleep."

"I can't leave my Mick."

"You're not doing anything for him now. He's in good hands. You'll be no use to him if you don't get any sleep yourself."

"Come on Lucy, you can come back to mine. I'll sleep on the sofa you can have the bed."

"I can't take your bed from you."

"Yes you can. It won't hurt me to be on the sofa for once. Your need is greater than mine."

Lucy gave a half hearted nod and left the room with Ellie.

The doctor followed them out and said, "We'll call you if there is any change for the worst."

Ellie got Lucy back to the flat and watched Lucy collapse on to the sofa leaning forward head in hands. Ellie sat down beside her and put an arm around her shoulder. She said nothing, knowing there were no words to help at that time.

Chapter Five

Lucy turned her head, hearing someone approach. It was Ellie.

"How is he," she asked.

"He's asleep," whispered Lucy.

"That's good. He needs to rest."

"That's what they keep telling me."

It had been a week since Mick had been admitted to hospital. He had come round, but spent most of the time asleep, which the staff said was good for him. It had been a nasty heart attack. When he got home he was going to have to slow down. It would be a long recovery time. Lucy was just glad she still had her husband. She would make sure he rested as much as possible. He would be wrapped in cotton wool between her and Ellie who had said she would help wherever possible.

Their latest detective work had been put on hold. The police had tried to speak to Ellie again but she had refused and explained what was happening. They had agreed to wait as they didn't expect to get much out of her anyway. It was just that she was the closest neighbour and had heard footsteps running away and a scream. Ellie had said she knew no more but they wanted to speak to her anyway in case their questioning brought anything else to mind.

Ellie was feeling strained without the police on her back. She was doing the work of two people as she and Lucy were the most experienced podiatrists there. The annoying thing was that Mick was in a different hospital which wasn't even close by. It would have been so much easier if it were the same place then Ellie could pop in during her lunch break.

Lucy couldn't be persuaded to leave Mick's side. Even though there was nothing she could do she refused to budge, except to go home to sleep. She would get there first thing in the morning and wouldn't leave until the evening. She ignored visiting times. The staff tolerated her. It couldn't be said why she was allowed to break the rules as they were usually very strict. She had been adamant she wouldn't leave and the staff feeling sorry for her had agreed. At first it was because they didn't expect Mick to survive but now he was awake and would be ok but Lucy still sat there.

"You don't need to keep coming you know," stated Lucy on Saturday.

"I want to be there for you both," responded Ellie. "You're my closest friend and I wouldn't be a very good one if I wasn't here when you need me most."

Lucy nodded, unable to fault Ellie's logic. Truth be told she was rather glad she wasn't on her own. She found the long hours boring as Mick slept most of the time. He tended to drop off mid sentence and Lucy couldn't help but worry. She had been told it was normal but she still couldn't switch off the anxiety. She felt if she were to leave him he might take a turn for the worst. She knew they would let her know if that were the case but was worried she wouldn't be there when he needed her most.

"He's sleeping why don't we go to the café downstairs and get a drink?"

"He might wake up and need me and I wouldn't be here," said Lucy.

Ellie was always trying to persuade Lucy to leave his bedside but nothing would drag her away. Lucy knew if she were needed and she wasn't there she would never forgive herself.

"Mick wouldn't want you wearing yourself out like this. You've barely eaten or slept this past week. You need to be strong for him but you'll be no use like this," said Ellie.

Lucy hardly heard, concentrating on Mick as she was. Any slight change and she wanted to pick up on it. Ellie shook her head, she was getting nowhere. Staff couldn't persuade her either. Ellie was at the stage where she was thinking of suggesting to staff that they call security to remove her at the end of visiting time. No one had the heart to force her to leave but it was becoming worrying, at least as far as Ellie was concerned.

Ellie decided to take positive action on the way out. She managed to catch the ward sister, "Excuse me, but I'm worried about my friend Lucy who won't leave Mick's side."

"Yes, I know we have expressed our concerns to her but she refuses to hear us."

"She'll make herself ill if she doesn't change this pattern soon. I was thinking she might be persuaded to leave if she were threatened with security at the end of visiting hours."

"That's a good idea, but I don't know if it will work. I'm reluctant to follow through if she still ignores me as it could backfire and make her worse and worry herself sick at home."

"I hadn't thought about that. If she came home with me though I could try and occupy her mind." Ellie paused before grinning and continued, "In fact I think I have just the thing, if it works that is."

"Ok I'll go and have a word with her now. If you can wait here for her."

"You sound confident you can do it."

"Just watch me."

Ellie stood there eyes on the sister as she strode purposefully down the ward to where Mick lay sleeping with Lucy holding his hand.

"Come on now love, visiting time is over and you really need some rest."

Lucy didn't take her eyes off Mick as she responded, "I can't leave him. He might need me."

"We're here to look after him and can meet his needs. If there were any change in his condition we know how to contact you."

Lucy shook her head, her vision becoming blurry as tears threatened to spill out. The sister saw this and her heart broke for this couple whose lives had changed in an instant, but she gave herself a mental shake. She couldn't back down now, it was vital for Lucy's wellbeing.

"I know it's difficult but you need to take care of yourself or you'll end up in a bed as a patient and then how will you be here for Mick."

"I can't leave him." Lucy was adamant on this one point.

"Ok, if that's the case I'm afraid I will have to take it further and call security. Come on your friend is waiting for you at the end of the ward. She's going to take you to hers so you're not on your own. You can come back tomorrow at visiting time."

"Please don't make me. I can't bear to leave him." Lucy suddenly felt nausea rise up into her throat and started retching.

"Come on dearie, let's go. You're in no fit state to stay here."

Lucy reluctantly stood and allowed the sister to lead her up the ward into Ellie's waiting arms.

"It's for the best," said Ellie as she nodded slightly at the sister not wanting Lucy to see there had been collaboration between them.

Chapter Six

It was the weekend. Lucy had done nothing but sleep and visit Mick the last few days. She had been unaware how tired she really was. She wasn't about to admit this though. She didn't want to hear I told you so's from anyone.

She sat up in bed and yawned. Looking at her phone to see the time she was it was only eight in the morning. This was the earliest she'd been awake for the last four days. She got up and went to the bathroom. Ellie hearing her moving around went through and said hello to her friend as she went back to the bedroom.

"You look better, you've even got colour in your cheeks."

"I feel it actually. I didn't realise how tired I really was."

"You did look terrible. Drastic action was needed."

"I can see that now. I can see the change in Mick as well that I couldn't see before when I was permanently with him. He is sleeping less and talks a bit when I'm there."

"That's very good. Well, now that you're up why don't we have a proper English breakfast."

"Bacon and egg? That sounds good," said Lucy realising how hungry she was.

"After that we should get some detective work going. We have the whole morning before visiting hours this afternoon."

"I don't know how much use I'll be, my thoughts are still on Mick. Anyway it doesn't seem right doing anything without his input and guidance."

"Come on, don't be a spoilsport. We're two strong, independent women we don't need a man to help us. We're the detective duo."

Lucy gave a weak smile and nodded. How could she resist? Besides it would be good to show Mick what they were capable of, plus she knew he would be interested in what was happening. It would be something to talk about when she visited him.

In the kitchen they got to cooking their breakfast. Ellie's mind was already on the mystery of the disappearing man, dead or alive, that she didn't notice the smoke coming from the frying pan and the burning bacon until the fire alarm went off. Ellie covered her face in embarrassment. How could she have done that. It had never happened before. She threw windows open to help get rid of all the steam then she left the flat to turn it off at the panel inside the main door. Downstairs she found Tammy just opening her door with a yawn.

"Sorry if I disturbed you," said Ellie. "I was cooking breakfast for me and my friend."

"It's ok," said Tammy. "I'm glad that's all it is. I'm not up to anything. I couldn't get to sleep last night and I only dropped off about an hour or so ago."

"I'm so sorry," apologised Ellie a second time. She felt so guilty as Tammy looked so tired and pale, more so than usual.

Tammy nearly fell. Ellie rushed forward and caught her. "Come on, I'll help you back to bed."

"No it's ok I can manage."

"No you can't. You nearly fell just now and I would only worry you will fall and be stuck on the floor with no one to help."

Tammy gave in and allowed Ellie to help her inside.

"I can see this is your bedroom," said Ellie seeing the open door that had been closed last time she had been there.

"It's ok I can manage now."

"No you're not. I'm seeing you into bed before I leave you."

"There is really no need."

Ellie was starting to wonder why Tammy wouldn't let her any further. How could she be acting so strange about a bedroom. All bedrooms were the same weren't they? A bed, wardrobe etc.

"I'm not leaving you before you're in bed," repeated Ellie.

Tammy seeing no help for it continued forward into the bedroom. Ellie at a quick glance saw straight away what the issue was. She was hard put not to gasp as she saw the skeleton standing in the corner of the room and a wall covered with paper with descriptions and suspects covering them. What was going on here. She couldn't help but shiver slightly, it was enough to give anyone the creeps. There was definitely more to Tammy than met the eye. Was she really as ill as she said she was? Could she have anything to do with Ashley's disappearance? She couldn't wait to get out of there and back to the relative normality of her own flat.

Tammy laid down and closed her eyes with a sigh of relief. She dozed straight away without even saying thank you or goodbye to Ellie. Ellie seeing she was ok left the flat and went back to her own.

"Are you all right?" asked Lucy seeing how pale her friend was. "You look as if you've seen a ghost."

"I feel as if I have," said Ellie sitting down quickly, feeling very shaky.

"What is it?"

"Tammy. She was outside her flat disturbed by the alarm. She nearly fell so I insisted on seeing her back to bed. You'll never believe what was in her bedroom...." Ellie paused before continuing. ".... A skeleton and all this weird stuff stuck to the walls. It was creepy."

"Sounds it."

"I think we have to consider whether she had something to do with Ashley's disappearance. After all she admitted to knowing him quite well. I'd just never got around to speaking to her about him because of everything that's been happening with Mick."

"It certainly gives us something to work on but we have to remember that there might not even be a problem. Ashley might be safe and well somewhere."

"I know, but I have my doubts. I think it's highly suspicious."

"If I think about it I have to agree with you."

Ellie was quietly congratulating herself. She had taken the focus away from Mick and on to something more mysterious. Lucy was looking animated as she thought about Ellie's findings.

"I think it explains the closed door," said Lucy.

"What do you mean?" asked Ellie blankly.

"You said the last time you were at Tammy's the bedroom door was shut."

Ellie shook her head to clear it. "Yes you're right. Sorry I was on another planet for a minute."

"Where were you?"

Ellie shrugged not wanting to reveal her thoughts. She didn't want Lucy's mind to go back to Mick.

"I think you need an excuse to go back to Tammy's. We need to find out exactly what is going on there as well as find out more about Ashley."

"I know but after what I saw I don't ever want to go back there, much less speak to her."

"You can't avoid her as that would make her suspicious."

"I don't think so since she is mostly indoors anyway. She has never phoned me for anything so it wouldn't seem strange. She's my number one suspect at the moment."

"Do I need to remind you she's our only suspect. We don't know Ashley or anything about his life. Without Tammy we're not going to get any further with this investigation."

"I see your point and I'm not ready to give up so I suppose I'll have to find an excuse to speak to her." Ellie shivered at the thought. She really had felt quite frightened when she saw the bedroom with all its paraphernalia. There was more to Tammy than met the eye. If Tammy had done away with Ashley who was supposed to be a friend what would she do to Ellie.

Ellie's phone rang interrupting her thoughts. "Hello……yes Tammy……I'll be there in a minute…..ok bye."

"What does she want?"

"She thinks she dropped her tablets but can't find them and she needs one. She says she's feeling very dizzy."

"Do you want me to come with you?"

Ellie shook her head. "Not a good idea as she could then bump us both off. At least if I don't return you can call the police."

"You're being a bit melodramatic aren't you."

"Maybe, I'm just really spooked. Anyway I'd better go."

"I'll wash up the breakfast things while you're gone."

"Great thanks. Wish me luck." With that Ellie was gone.

Lucy was left with her thoughts which inevitably went back to the subject of Mick. She wondered how he was. She would have loved to talk over the latest findings but knew he had to take it easy without stress of any sort. Anyway she wasn't sure there was much of significance to tell him as yet. She sighed. She couldn't wait to get him home but knew it wouldn't happen just yet, but she gained some comfort to know he was improving bit by bit. He was awake more and becoming more alert with each day that passed.

………

Ellie managed to get into Tammy's flat and went straight to the bedroom, knocking first and calling to say who it was. On being given permission to enter she went in. She had to steel herself for what was to come, sure it couldn't be anything good.

"Hi Ellie, sorry to ring you but I really need a tablet but I dropped it. It's definitely here somewhere," said Tammy in a voice which sounded weak and as if much effort was required just to get a single word out.

"What does it look like?"

"Pink and very small. It could be anywhere."

"OK, this may take some time then."

Ellie started by searching the bed as that seemed the most likely place for it to be. Tammy was just about able to turn herself over for Ellie to see if she was laying on it. No tablet in the bed or under the pillows. Tammy lay back utterly exhausted by moving slightly and lifting her head up. She closed her eyes and allowed Ellie to continue searching in silence.

Ellie took the opportunity to surreptitiously take a closer look at the papers stuck to the wall. She was horrified to see Ashley's name written on one in large letters. There were arrows below pointing to other names. Ellie wished she could ask what it all meant, but didn't dare. Although Tammy looked too ill and weak to hurt a fly she wasn't taking any chances. It was obvious though that Tammy knew quite a bit about Ashley's life and was acquainted with people in it. She knew Ashley better than she had led Ellie to believe.

As Ellie continued to search she started having doubts as to the validity of Tammy's reason for getting her down there. Surely the tablet would be there somewhere and would have been found much easier. With this thought came fear. If it was some sort of ruse to get her in the flat what was her real motive. Was Ellie herself in danger?

"I'm sorry I can't find it anywhere. I think you're better off getting another one out."

"It's got to be somewhere," protested Tammy.

"Well ok if you insist," said Ellie doubtfully.

Tammy hadn't done anything threatening so far but you never could tell. It could all be part of the plan. Why did she want Ellie to stay there instead of giving up and leaving? It wasn't as if she were making any attempt at conversation.

There it was. Ellie gave a shout of triumph and rushed over to the skeleton. She gave a shiver as she brushed against it. It definitely gave her the creeps.

Picking up the tablet she passed it to Tammy who was so grateful, over the top considering it was only a tablet. Anyone would think she had just got hold of the crown jewels or something equally valuable or maybe won the lottery.

"I'm glad I could help," Ellie whispered and made to leave the room.

"Please don't go. I want to tell you something."

"I can't stay this time, I'm sorry but I've got a friend staying at the moment and I must get back to her."

Tammy nodded, disappointment showing on her face, that made Ellie feel guilty for leaving, but she couldn't stay in that room any longer.

"Look I'll try and pop in tomorrow. It's Sunday so I'll be home all day. How about I bring my friend with me. Will you be able to cope with the two of us."

Tammy gave a weak smile and nodded her agreement but said nothing.

"That's settled then. We'll see you tomorrow probably late morning."

Tammy nodded and closed her eyes. It was probably for the best anyway she really was having a bad day.

………..

"I had a good look around while I was in there. Ashley's name was on a piece of paper with arrows pointing to other names. It seems that Tammy must be caught up in this somehow."

"Maybe we'll find out something tomorrow, you said she wanted to see us."

Ellie nodded.

"There is something I want to query though, how do you know there is anything suspicious about Ashley's disappearance? Without a body we actually know nothing. Can we be totally one hundred percent certain that there has been some wrongdoing here. All we've got is a potentially missing person and a red bath which could be anything – even paint. We are only assuming it's blood. There could be an innocent explanation," said Lucy trying to bring Ellie back to reality.

"I know you're right but it does seem suspicious when Tammy has all that information written down."

"Maybe, but it doesn't really mean anything."

Lucy agreed with Ellie about the whole strange affair but just wanted to play devils advocate to see what came into their minds. It could bring about a revelation or nothing at all.

"We do know the skeleton can't be Ashley as he hasn't been missing long enough to decompose like that," said Ellie.

"Are you suggesting there has been another dead body that we don't know about?"

"No, oh I don't know what I think. All I know is that room gives me the creeps."

"Maybe I'll get to see it tomorrow and then we can compare our thoughts when we get back."

"Sounds a great idea."

"Did you by any chance get to remember any of the names which appear to be linked to Ashley?"

Ellie shook her head, "I didn't pay much attention. I was too spooked for that."

"I can understand," said Lucy. There was silence before she continued, "I suppose Ashley is his real name and Tammy hasn't just made it up to put us and the police off the scent."

"That hadn't even occurred to me. That really would confuse the issue further."

"Do we know what she's told the police?"

"I don't know if the police have spoken to her yet. She hasn't made any comment."

"But why would she? Especially if she's as guilty as we're thinking. Besides she's hardly likely to confide in you when she barely knows you and doesn't know about our private detective business on the side."

"You're making perfect sense as usual."

"Of course I am. I have to reign you in for your own good sometimes."

"I agree entirely with that. I would be seeing dead bodies everywhere, even when there are none."

"I know we got involved and solved Phyllis's murder last year but that doesn't mean we can do the same with others. It was just that we knew the people involved last time. This time and any time in the future we won't. Then we would just be sticking out nose in when it isn't wanted. It's very difficult to carry out an investigation when we don't know the people involved and their motives.

Chapter Seven

Ellie knocked on the door and waited. When no one answered Ellie turned to Lucy saying, "Well she should be in. She knew we were coming at this time. Anyway she never goes out."

"Maybe she's in the loo or something. She can't help that," said Lucy as reasonable as always.

"Maybe the police have arrested her?"

"What for?"

"Murder."

"With evidence?"

Ellie shrugged. "Who knows, they may have everything they need to make an arrest. Case closed."

"If you say so. Except they haven't been around much or we would have heard something as it would have become much busier. It's so quiet, it couldn't happen without us hearing or seeing something."

"You've got a point there. I'm worried. I hope she's ok."

It was at that moment the door opened and Tammy greeted them. She still looked very pale and was clinging on to the door for support as if she would fall, which perhaps she would. She was extremely frail in appearance.

"Hi Tammy this is my friend Lucy."

"Hi Lucy," said a voice that was barely above a whisper.

"Look are you sure you're well enough for visitors. You seem very frail today," commented Ellie.

"Please come in."

They entered and Ellie's eyes automatically went to the bedroom which had the door shut again. Ellie couldn't understand it as she had been in there. Tammy noticed Ellie's eyes going there but said nothing. The reality was she liked some privacy and that was her bedroom. Her private space. She was used to people going in and out but was determined they wouldn't see her in there.

"Take a seat," Tammy said to the friends. "Tea? Coffee?"

"Let me make it," said Ellie. "You look as if you're ready to drop."

Tammy didn't even try to protest. She did as she was told and took a seat, giving Lucy a weak smile as she did so.

"Sorry, I'm not usually as bad as this."

"Don't worry about it. We understand."

"More than most people do. They don't want to get it and think I'm just lazy and work shy."

"That's terrible," said Lucy. "I can promise you we don't think that at all."

Ellie took the teas through on a tray to avoid going back and forth. She placed them on a low coffee table and handed them out. There was silence as they slowly sipped the hot liquid.

"I'm really worried," said Tammy.

"What about?" asked Ellie. "Maybe we can help in some way."

"I'm not sure how. You barely knew him."

Ellie and Lucy exchanged subtle glances. Were they about to get some information or a way in to ask the right questions?

"Who?" asked Ellie, deciding it might be better for her to take the lead as she lived there and was involved in finding the bath in the state that it was in. It could have been odd if Lucy were asking the questions.

"Ashley. He's never away this long and the day before his disappearance he was in here visiting me and said things."

"Like what?"

"He thought he was being followed for one thing."

"Did he see the person?"

"He caught glimpses of them every now and again."

"Gender?"

"He wasn't sure as it was just the odd glance. They appeared to be very good at hiding themselves."

"Was he scared?"

Tammy nodded, taking another sip of her tea.

"Could Ashley have just gone away for a while to shake off the unwanted attention?"

"I hadn't thought of that. No, he'd have told me if that was the case. I always knew when he was away."

"Maybe he decided it would be safer not to tell anyone."

"That way anyone following him wouldn't find out where he was."

"If he was that scared he wouldn't want to put you in danger as well," said Lucy, speaking for the first time.

"You could be right I suppose. I'm not convinced though."

"Did he ever mention any friends or family he was in touch with. Maybe phone calls need to be made to verify what is going on."

"I couldn't do that," said Tammy looking horrified at the mere thought.

"That's ok I'd be happy to do it," said Ellie.

"Would people be willing to answer you truthfully though when they don't know you. They might be a bit cagey especially if Ashley really is missing."

"You have a point there," said Lucy. "But I don't think there is any choice. We need to find out what's happened as soon as possible. You can count on us."

"Thank you so much. I thought that would be the case. I couldn't help but notice you looking hard at the images and words up on my wall yesterday. I usually keep my door closed so no one can see. I like to make notes of specific cases and then work on it in my head just to see if I can get the solution. Something to use my brain about to stop it atrophying."

"Good thinking." Ellie was impressed with Tammy's logic. "You can trust us. This isn't the first case of murder we've solved."

"Murder?! You think it's murder then?"

Ellie could have bitten her tongue off. She'd said too much and now if Tammy were involved in anyway they were both in danger. Good job she'd made the tea or Tammy might put something in it to poison them. A nice easy way of murder that could be anyone, but wouldn't take much energy to carry out.

………

"Well," said Lucy when they were safely back in Ellie's flat. "What did you make of that."

"It was all a bit weird and muddled."

"Seeing her like that though I think poison would be the only way for her to commit murder. She doesn't look as if she's got the strength to do anything too practical like drowning him. It's either not Tammy or there isn't a problem to start with. Full stop."

"And we still don't know why she has a skeleton in her room or why she decided to investigate when she seemed so surprised when we mentioned murder."

"A lot of contradictions certainly. I don't know where we can take it from as we still don't have any information."

"I remember seeing the name Belinda written down."

"Girlfriend perhaps? Although we can't do anything with it when we have no details for her. I think we have no choice but to leave this to the police this time."

"Hmm," said Ellie reluctantly. "I still think we can look into it."

"How?"

Ellie shrugged. "I really have no idea."

"Exactly my point."

At that moment Ellie's phone rang.

"Hello is that Ellie Strange?"

"Speaking….. yes…. Ok that's fine, I can do that….see you in a while."

Disconnecting the call, Ellie turned to Lucy and said, "Police. They want me to go down to the station and answer some questions about Ashley I think."

"I'll come with you," said Lucy standing up to get her coat. Ellie did the same.

Wrapped up warm as the temperatures were still bitterly cold although the snow had gone they went out to the car. Lucy was shivering as she got in the drivers side. They would take her car. Quickly putting the heating on they set off. At least she hadn't had to scrape the windscreen, that was something.

They made the journey in near silence as Ellie was apprehensive, wondering why they had to go to the station when she was only a neighbour who had called them. She didn't have any information.

"I'm sure it's just routine," said Lucy, seeing the frown on Ellie's face.

"I hope so," said Ellie.

………..

"Come in and take a seat," said Sergeant Bronson.

Ellie sat down. She felt at a disadvantage as there was two officers and her. Lucy hadn't been allowed in and was currently sitting in reception waiting nervously for her friend.

"We're recording this," said the sergeant and introduced his colleague as Constable Clown.

Ordinarily she and Lucy would have a good laugh about the name and maybe they would at a later date but right now laughing was the last thing she felt like doing. Nausea was welling up inside. She swallowed hoping not to embarrass herself like that.

"Try and relax," said Constable Clown, noticing the tension which was emanating from her.

Ellie took a few deep breaths but still felt rigid with anxiety. She had never been interviewed formally before and was worried about what they thought they knew.

"Ok let's begin," said Sergeant Bronson, impatient to get to the point. He had little empathy for people he was interviewing, assuming they were guilty unless proven otherwise. He knew this wasn't the right way round but couldn't help the way he thought. He was very much old school in his thinking.

"You made the 999 call on the day your neighbour disappeared. Can you explain why?"

"The bath had what looked like blood in it and I had heard a scream and running feet."

"Do you know who it was."

Ellie shook her head, "They had disappeared by the time I left my flat."

"Male or female?"

"I think male because the footsteps sounded heavy and outside there were largish footprints in the snow."

The constable nodded, hoping to convey a level of understanding.

"What made you look at the footprints?"

"I'm a podiatrist so interested in anything to do with feet."

"A podiatrist not a police officer I notice. Why then would footprints interest you? You're not involved in forensics so they would mean nothing to you."

"They help identify the gender of the person as I have just said," said Ellie, trying to sound more confident than she felt. She was actually quite intimidated by the sergeant asking the questions.

"What do you know about your neighbour?"

"Nothing really. We've just said hello in passing but that isn't often."

"How do you know his name then?"

"The neighbour downstairs knows him quite well and mentioned his name as being Ashley."

The sergeant nodded.

"Can you describe him?"

Ellie had to think about this before saying, "Tall, dark hair, big feet, a size 10 I would guess."

"How can you know that?"

"I'm a podiatrist remember. It's my job."

"To know peoples shoe size?" Sergeant Bronson was very sceptical. He was becoming sure that Ellie knew Ashley better than she was leading them to believe.

"I can usually guess and am quite accurate at it as well."

"When was the last time you saw Ashley?"

Ellie was quiet for some minutes as she thought about it. "Sorry I can't remember. It must have been some time ago. I didn't see him but heard him shouting."

"At whom?"

"I really don't know as I know nothing about his life."

"Surely you knew if it was a male or female voice," said Sergeant Bronson who really felt that Ellie was being deliberately evasive.

"I heard no other voice, but if he was on the phone I wouldn't."

"Or maybe it was you and you don't want to admit it."

Ellie was stunned. Whatever she felt about the sergeant she certainly hadn't expected that.

"It wasn't me. I don't know him enough to argue about anything."

"Hmm," said the sergeant, not believing this for one minute.

"Let's say that you've got information from your downstairs neighbour, what have you got from her?"

"He is involved somehow with someone called Belinda. I don't know who she is."

"Your neighbour didn't say?"

"I saw it written on a sheet of paper," said Ellie seeing no help for it but to tell them everything she knew. She went on to tell them all she had seen in Tammy's bedroom including the skeleton.

"Why would she have all that documented if she's not connected with us and is as ill as you say she is?"

"I don't know. We thought it odd as well. In fact we considered she might be guilty."

"Guilty of what?"

"Murder."

Sergeant Bronson raised his eyebrows at this. No one had mentioned murder so why would Ellie when she insisted she knew nothing about the case.

"How do you know it was murder?"

Ellie blushed and said, "Well, he disappeared and there was blood around."

"Doesn't mean anything."

The two officers looked at each other unsure what to make of Ellie who seemed to know too much but at the same time was giving nothing away. Even the constable was getting suspicious now.

Sergeant Bronson looked at his watch and looked at his colleague who nodded. "You can go for now but be available if we need to ask you anything further."

"But why? I haven't done anything. I don't even know anything."

"We'll see."

They led her out to the reception area where an anxious Lucy was waiting.

"There you are! I thought they'd arrested you or something."

"I thought they were going to."

"What! I was only joking."

"I'm not unfortunately."

"Come on let's go home and I'll make you a nice cup of tea." Lucy took Ellie's arm and led her out of the station and back to the car.

Getting in the car Ellie was unable to keep it in any longer and burst into tears. Lucy leaned across and took Ellie's hand and held it while she cried.

"It was......it was......awful......" Ellie sobbed unable to say more.

…………..

Once back home Ellie collapsed on to the sofa, shaken from the tears and the interview.

"Lucy I think I'm a suspect. They didn't seem to believe that I really know nothing. I was expected to know who Ashley was arguing with and details about his life. He was just my neighbour for goodness sake."

"You sound angry now. That's good. You had me worried for a while there."

Ellie sipped the hot tea gratefully. "Thanks. That's a nice cup of tea."

I know how you like it." There was a pause before Lucy continued, "I've just had a thought did you tell them about Tammy?"

"Of course I did but I'm not sure they took any notice. I said we'd suspected her of murder."

"They looked taken aback."

"I'm not surprised. What made you say that? We don't even know it was murder as there's no body as yet."

Ellie put her head in her hands. Looking up again she said, "I didn't even think. I don't think I was capable of coherent thought by then. I was just desperately trying to think of something to take there thoughts away from me."

"I can understand that. You sound as if you had a terrible time. I don't know how I would have coped if it had been me."

"Look can we change the subject. I really don't want to talk about it any further. It was too horrible to contemplate. It has made me want to know what really happened though or I can see myself being charged with something."

"How was Mrs Botts when you saw her the other day? I haven't seen her for a while," said Lucy changing the subject.

"She was fine. Opinionated as usual."

Lucy laughed. "I can imagine. She'll be telling us how to do our job soon."

"She already is."

"Come on spill the beans."

"Ok. Well I was cutting her nails as usual when she yelled. She was convinced I was cutting half way down her toe or at least that was the way it sounded. She told me I was going too low when I stopped. I hadn't even cut at that point I was just preparing to. Anyway, she let me get on with the job. I finished the rest without incident but then she insisted I hadn't cut some low enough. Others were too low. I don't know what she expected me to do I couldn't exactly put them back on. Stick them with super glue maybe."

Lucy couldn't help but laugh at this account. It sounded about right for the elderly lady. "She is funny even when she's being serious. I do like her."

"Yes so do I. I think I'll suggest next time that she cuts her own nails and I'll watch and learn how she wants them done."

"Good idea. I wonder what she'll say to that. It's bound to be something funny."

"I know. She does have a good sense of humour. I must remember to try it."

Lucy pleased to see Ellie's face lit up with amusement at the change of subject which was as Lucy had intended.

Ellie's phone rang, she answered it and sobered up as she listened.

Putting the phone down she turned to Lucy, "That was Tammy, she wants us to go for a cup of tea."

"Hmm. Wonder what she wants this time."

"I don't know, but I intend asking questions of her this time. I'm not going to be fobbed off by her illness, not now the police are zooming in on me."

"Good for you. I'll back you up you know that."

"Thanks. I know I can always count on you."

Talking as they went they were soon in Tammy's flat drinking a cup of tea. Lucy felt as if she would be swimming in it having just had one with Ellie before the phone call. There was silence for a while, each one not able to think what to say.

Tammy had just been feeling lonely and was keen to get to know the two women and become friends. She thought they would be good people to know. She occasionally heard outbursts of laughter coming from the flat and yearned to be part of it. She realised it could be difficult as they had known each other years and might not let someone else into the inner sanctum as she saw it.

Ellie and Lucy exchanged glances unsure how to approach the topic of Ashley.

"Have you heard anything from Ashley?" asked Ellie in the end.

Tammy shook her head but said nothing.

"You mentioned murder the other day. What made you think of that?"

"It's just that it's unusual for him to be away this long. He would have told me if it were so. He was always popping in for a chat so not to see him would be strange."

"You know him well then?"

Tammy nodded.

"Do you have any idea where he might be if he had gone of his own free will? Somewhere he knew well and liked?"

"He hardly ever went away. Even when not working or at college he still stayed at home."

"What about his family? Didn't he ever go and see them?"

"He had no family. He was in foster care for as long as he could remember. He never sees them, hasn't done since he left the system. He didn't like them that much. They looked after him well enough but there was no emotional attachment. He thought they would be glad to get rid of him when the time came. He left and gave them no forwarding address."

"Girlfriend?"

Tammy nodded. "He had a steady girlfriend. They'd been together for three years and were still as much in love as when they started going out."

"Do you have a name?"

"Belinda."

"Do you have any details for her? Maybe Ashley's there."

"It's possible I suppose but as I've already said, unlikely, as he would have told me if he was going away or moving out."

"How about you give us Belinda's phone number or address and we'll get in touch and see what she knows."

Tammy stayed silent, not knowing what to say. She wasn't sure Belinda would like her giving details away to people she doesn't know.

"I'm not sure. Belinda might not like it."

"Could you contact her and ask her the questions? We could write down things we can think of."

"I'm not sure I'm well enough for that."

Lucy and Ellie glanced at each other. What was going on? Surely if Tammy were able to see them she could phone Belinda and ask a couple of questions.

"Well maybe tomorrow if it's another good day."

"If today's a good day why not phone now and then we'll leave you to rest quietly."

"I'm running out of energy fast," said Tammy. She had thought these two women understood her illness or at least were prepared to accept but now she wasn't so sure.

"If you're getting tired we'll leave now. Let us know when you've spoken to Belinda. If you really can't just ask if we can talk to her and then give us her details," said Ellie standing up.

Chapter Eight

Ellie and Lucy sat in the café where they were to meet Belinda. Ellie looked at her watch and spoke, "She's ten minutes late, do you think she'll turn up."

"I don't know. Maybe she's the sort of person who's always late."

"Could be. Well let's give her a bit longer."

At that point a lady entered looking around uncertainly. Ellie stood up and asked, "Are you Belinda?"

The lady nodded shyly and sat down at the table.

"We're Ellie and Lucy here is my friend. Thanks for agreeing to meet us."

"That's ok. Can I get a drink before we talk. I'm gasping."

"Of course," said Ellie. Turning to Lucy, Ellie raised her eyebrows conveying a silent message to her friend. Were they even going to get anything out of Belinda. She seemed very quiet and had so far made no eye contact with them.

Taking small sips of her coffee Belinda sat there, quietly, so far not speaking. Ellie and Lucy began to feel quite uncomfortable, not knowing what to say. Had Tammy made a mistake? They couldn't imagine this quiet lady having a boyfriend, after all she never spoke. How could she have got to know Ashley and he her?

Ellie decided to take the plunge after glancing at Lucy and seeing her give a slight nod. "Belinda, Tammy told us you are close to Ashley who is my neighbour."

Belinda nodded but didn't open her mouth.

"Do you know where he is? We're concerned that he is hurt as there was blood in the bath and he's disappeared."

Belinda looked up in surprise, "How did you know that?"

"I heard a scream and feet running down the stairs. I went into the flat and found what looked like blood in the bath. I'm the one who phoned the police."

"The police haven't spoken to me."

"They probably don't know about you as Tammy only just told us. Apparently she knows Ashley quite well and is worried about his wellbeing."

"I'm his girlfriend. Or I was."

"What do you mean? You either are or you aren't," said Lucy coming into the conversation for the first time.

Tears sprung up into Belinda's eyes. "I don't know. He was behaving oddly for about a week before he disappeared. It was as if….Oh I don't know."

"As if what?" asked Ellie.

"I don't know. He seemed to be distancing himself from me and was talking about going away for a while. His plans didn't include me. I sort of thought it might be his way of breaking up with me."

"I'm sorry to hear that," said Lucy.

"Thank you."

"Do you know where he was thinking of going?" asked Ellie.

"No, he didn't say."

"It must be hard."

"It is. It hadn't occurred to me that he was in any sort of trouble. I thought it was just a holiday. Now I've spoken to you I'm worried as well. He does seem to have disappeared without trace."

Ellie and Lucy looked at each other and Ellie raised her eyebrows slightly, querying what she was hearing. Lucy shrugged, also unsure as to the truth of Belinda's statement.

"Did he do this often?" asked Lucy.

Belinda shook her head. "Never. He sometimes went to his parents without me but he always told me."

"Did you meet them?"

"Never. He always made some excuse why I couldn't go with him."

"Didn't it seem odd to you?"

"No. I just assumed they were in poor health. At least that's what he led me to believe."

"Do you have their contact details. Maybe he's there and perfectly safe."

"Even if I knew them why should I tell you. You are both strangers, just a neighbour of Ashley's. You clearly didn't know him well, if at all or you would have known me. You had to go through Tammy whom I know to be a close friend of Ashley's."

"You've got a point there. We're just two busybodies poking our noses in out of concern for Ashley."

Belinda nodded but said nothing.

"Where did he work?" asked Ellie.

Belinda said nothing.

"Please help us out. We have only his best interests at heart."

Again Belinda kept quiet. She drank the last of her coffee and stood up ready to leave.

Ellie and Lucy stood up as well, seeing the conversation was at an end and they were going to find out nothing more from her.

When she'd left Lucy turned to Ellie saying, "Well that wasn't very helpful. She gave nothing away. In fact she was quite evasive. I'm not sure I believe what she was saying. I think she knows more than she's letting on."

"I agree. I don't really know what to make of her."

"Neither did I. She was behaving very cagey if you ask me."

"Exactly. Well it's pointless sitting here why don't we leave as well. I wouldn't mind having another chat with Tammy. I think she knows more than she's letting on."

"Maybe we should drop in on her when we get back. Take her by surprise. That way she won't have answers sorted out in her head."

They agreed that's what they would do and Ellie drove them home.

Ellie knocked on the door and they waited. They waited a bit longer but nothing.

"Surely she can't be out," said Lucy. "I thought she was housebound."

"So did I. Maybe she just isn't up to visitors at the moment or is asleep."

"Well we're achieving nothing by standing here like idiots we might as well go indoors in the warm."

They made their way up to Ellie's flat and Lucy collapsed on to the sofa and closed her eyes.

"Are you ok?" asked Ellie with some concern.

"I've got a bit of a headache that's all."

"Why don't you go and have a lay down."

"I think I will."

Lucy went through to her room and laid down leaving Ellie on the sofa lost in thought. She was sure there was something strange going on with Ashley. Belinda and Tammy could well be in on it, depending what it was of course. Was Ashley even in danger? Was it possible that Belinda killed him believing him to be breaking up with her. That's if she was telling the truth about that. Tammy would surely have known that and she hadn't said. There definitely was some mystery surrounding her neighbour and his disappearance. Ellie wasn't sure what the truth was and they seemed very far from finding out. She was sure of one thing though, and that was Ashley was dead, killed by someone but who? She wished she could find out more about his life and the people in it. For instance what did he do for a living? What about colleagues? Were they guilty or another girlfriend that Belinda had alluded to?

The phone rung and Ellie picked it up quickly hoping not to disturb Lucy. She saw it was Tammy so she took the call.

"Did you knock a while ago?" asked Tammy coming straight to the point.

"Yes we did."

"Sorry I was resting. I always rest for an hour after lunch and I don't allow any disturbances during that time."

"Sorry if we woke you."

"You didn't. I was awake. I had hoped to sleep but it didn't happen. I hate it when I can't sleep, just lay there tossing and turning. I'm so tired but it wasn't to be."

"Belinda wasn't very helpful. That's an understatement. She said she knew nothing and went as far as to say Ashley had broken up with her."

"Had he? He didn't tell me that. Very odd, he used to tell me everything."

"Hmm," murmured Ellie, unsure who to believe as there was a mass of contradictions. Nothing made much sense.

"You don't believe me."

"It's not that, it's that there are different stories floating about. She also said Ashley spent quite a bit of time with his parents who are unwell."

"Really? That's odd," said Tammy. "He told me his parents are dead and he was brought up in care."

"Is it Ashley that's telling tales for some reason or is it Belinda."

"Or me," commented Tammy. "You must think that as a possibility."

"I wasn't going to say that."

"Thank you."

"Look I'll leave you to rest now. I don't want you to get over tired." On that note, Ellie disconnected the call, feeling more confused than ever. It just didn't make sense. Both ladies sounded very plausible but couldn't both be telling the truth. Unless of course, Ashley was telling stories to one or both of them. After all his life could be very complicated and she didn't really know him. Maybe his name wasn't even Ashley. If only they could find out where he worked but neither Tammy nor Belinda were forthcoming on that one.

"That was Tammy on the phone," said Ellie seeing Lucy coming back through.

"I thought it sounded as if it was from what you were saying. Did you find anything else out?"

"No, not really, just contradictions." Ellie went on to update Lucy on the phone conversation with Tammy.

"Very weird," commented Lucy.

"I know. Who do we believe? Is it even possible they are both lying for their own reasons? Or did Ashley lie to them both."

"Who knows."

I wish I had known Ashley and made the effort to get to know him while he lived next door. I don't even know what he did for a job."

"Even if we did know where he worked would it help us? I can't see his employer talking to us about him and his relationships with colleagues. He doesn't know us and we're not any official body that he would be obliged to help."

"I see your point. Where does this leave us now?"

"I really don't know."

Chapter Eight

"Hello Mick," said Lucy rushing to his bedside. "It's good to see you sat out. You must be feeling better."

"I didn't want to get out at first I must admit, but when I was sitting here I felt better about it. It must mean I'm getting better don't you think?"

"Definitely."

"Anyway, enough of my health what's been happening with you two? I hope you've been staying out of mischief."

"Is that possible?"

"Well now I think about it I don't think it is."

"We met up with Belinda, Ashley's girlfriend according to Tammy."

"And?" queried Mick.

"It was all very odd. Belinda seemed to think they had broken up and talked about Ashley going to his parents a lot but Tammy says the opposite and actually told us that Ashley's parents are dead."

"How weird."

"That's exactly what we thought."

There was silence as Mick gave the matter some thought. "You know something, I think it is possible that Tammy was told he never sees his parents for some reason only Ashley knows and she interpreted it as being his parents died."

"That doesn't make sense," said Lucy, before adding, "There is also still the matter that Belinda says he goes to see his parents quite a lot. If Tammy were as close to him as she claims she would know that as well."

"Then if Ashley didn't lie then one of the ladies is lying to you."

"That's something we do agree on. But why lie?"

"That we can't know until we have more pieces of the puzzle. We don't really know anything yet. I think we need to know more about Belinda and her motives. That could be your next question for Tammy."

Lucy nodded. "Belinda seemed very quiet, reluctant to talk to us. We had to almost drag information out of her."

"That could be suspicious in itself."

"We didn't think of it like that. We just assumed it was her personality as we even thought it odd Belinda was able to have a boyfriend when she makes no effort to communicate with us. It was just very straight to the point with her."

"So you couldn't get to know her as a person then."

Lucy shook her head.

"It could have been an act, had you thought of that?"

Again Lucy shook her head and said, "Not once did it cross our minds we just thought it was her."

"See what else you can find out from Tammy. It's highly likely she knows more than she's letting on about Belinda. If she was close to Ashley as she claims then she must have known about his girlfriend from what Ashley said."

"You've got a point there but we aren't getting far with speaking to her. She claims to be too unwell to talk suddenly."

"You don't think it's genuine."

"Not sure."

"The sooner I'm out of this place the better then we can talk it over easier and I can see where we need to go from here."

"Oh no you don't. You need to rest when you get out of here. No work that's what the doctor told you."

"I will be resting. I can look over your notes and see what comes to mind. I'm not brain dead you know. It was my heart not my head."

"I know that, but I'm not risking you ending up back in here again."

"I won't. I've had enough of this place. I've been here too long."

"Have they said how much longer you might be here."

Mike shook his head. "I've tried asking but they have been quite evasive."

"Ok I'll try asking when I leave. Hopefully it will be soon."

"Oh I hope so, I'm starting to go stir crazy."

"Not as much as me. I refused to leave the place when you were first in here."

"I didn't know that."

"You wouldn't you were out of it most of the time. We didn't know if you would make it."

"Was I that bad?"

Lucy nodded.

"I didn't realise."

"How could you when you were unconscious and later sleeping all the time."

"I knew it was a bad heart attack but…." Mick went silent as he thought back. No memories came to him of that difficult time when it was touch and go.

"Anyway I suppose I should leave you to rest before I'm thrown out of here."

Mick leaned forward for his goodbye kiss which wasn't long in coming.

Lucy stopped to speak to the nurse as she'd said she would do.

The nurse shook her head. "The doctor hasn't said anything about discharge so it won't be yet. He is stable now but we're not taking any chances of another heart attack occurring."

"Is that likely?"

"Yes."

Lucy went pale. It hadn't even occurred to her that her beloved husband might have another one.

"Sorry, I seem to have given you a shock. I thought you would have known."

Lucy shook her head, unable to respond.

"Look sit down while I get you a cup of tea. You look like you need one."

"Why is tea always offered as the solution to all ills?"

"Sorry I thought it would help."

"Stop apologising," snapped Lucy.

"Look why don't I get someone who might know more than I do."

Lucy shook her head. "I just want to go home now."

Lucy knew she wasn't being very polite but seemed incapable of being nice. She realised it wasn't the nurse's fault. She was just the one in the way.

Lucy left the hospital and made her way back to Ellie's where she was still spending all her time. She drove slowly aware that her concentration wasn't as it should be and wanted to avoid an accident.

She arrived home without any incident much to her relief and went inside.

"Are you all right?" asked Ellie, immediately concerned for her friend.

"I had a shock that's all."

"Is it Mick?"

"Well sort of. I asked the nurse when he could come home and she didn't know but said they were monitoring him closely in case he should have another heart attack."

Ellie drew Lucy to her in a hug, wanting to offer some comfort. "I'm sure he'll be fine. He's out of danger now isn't he."

"Well yes but…I don't know what I'm trying to say. I'm so worried."

"Of course you are. It's understandable. It doesn't help when you don't know the exact situation."

"That's partly my fault. The nurse did suggest getting someone to speak to me but I refused. I just needed to get out of there."

"I can understand that. It must come as a shock. Maybe tomorrow we can speak to someone who knows what they are talking about."

"We?"

"Yes, I'm coming with you so we can face it together."

"Thank you. You're a good friend."

"Well of course. We've known each other a long time."

"I don't even know how many years it is."

"Neither do I. We met at college when we started our training and we've been friends ever since."

"Much to the dismay of supervisors especially Phyllis."

"Don't mention her. I still see her lying at the bottom of the stairs dead. I always shudder when we use the stairs."

"Fortunately that's not often because I'm too lazy to climb stairs when we can use the lift."

"I'm the same. The lift suits me fine."

"I suppose we should use the stairs as it would be a bit of exercise."

"That would be enough exercise for the day."

"Agreed."

"We always agree on that. We are both lazy buggers." The pair burst into laughter. It felt good to laugh, having had nothing to laugh about for some time, what with Ashley disappearing and Mick's heart attack the last few weeks had been pretty grim.

They settled down and leaned back comfortably on the sofa. "I needed that," said Lucy.

"Me too."

"What do you think we should do now?"

"I'm not sure. I think going and checking Ashley's flat would be good," said Ellie.

"But that would be breaking and entering. What if we get caught?"

"What choice have we got? Tammy and Belinda are contradicting each other and possibly holding something back. There is a chance we could find out more if we search the flat. Maybe something about his job."

"I'm not sure. If we get caught....I need to be available for Mick not in prison. Plus if we want to continue working we can't afford to have a criminal record."

"You've got a point, but who's going to catch us. If Tammy did she won't do anything as she has been helping or pretending to help us. If you don't want to come with me I understand but I'll take the risk."

"Me let you go alone? No way, we're in this together. We're the private investigator duo. Where you go I go, even if it is to keep you out of trouble."

"Great." Ellie grinned at her friend. She had been sure all along that Lucy would join her. They were inseparable as Mick had often commented.

Chapter Nine

"Well we're in. To be quite honest I'll never know how you manage it but I'm probably better off not knowing."

"I can show you and write instructions down so you can do it if needs be."

Lucy shook her head. "It's all right. I think I'd rather remain in ignorance. I've got you if ever I need to break the law. Now come on we better get to it. Being in here makes me nervous. What's the plan since this was your idea."

"I didn't have one," said Ellie sounding a bit sheepish.

"What are we doing here then. You should have had a plan worked out in your mind before we came. We don't want to waste time discussing it. It gives more time for the police to show up."

"I know. Sorry I didn't think. I just thought we should search."

"What are we searching for exactly?"

Ellie shrugged. "I don't know. Anything that might give us a clue where to go from here. Or maybe something that will show who's lying to us."

"Ok then, I'll take the kitchen while you do the bedroom. We'll do the living room together since that's the biggest room."

Ellie nodded, secretly relieved that Lucy was taking charge. She did feel a bit stupid not having a plan worked out, but Lucy was making sense.

They split up and went their separate ways to see what they could come up with.

Ellie was methodically taking everything out of the drawers with the intention of putting things back the same way she'd found them. This was important as it seemed as if he was a neat freak. Everything was in order and very tidy. When it came to the underwear drawer Ellie wasn't sure she wanted to delve through it but knew she had to if she were to do this properly.

She got to the bottom, it all emptied out except for a folder of some sort. Ellie got excited, sure it must be of some importance considering it was in the underwear drawer full of boxer shorts. She sat on the bed and opened it. She found photos placed inside with a date and brief note what was in the photo and where it was taken.

Ellie looked through it and couldn't understand why it should be hidden away. It just seemed an ordinary album to her, nothing top secret.

"Hey, there's no time for slacking," said Lucy who had gone looking for Ellie having finished her search of the kitchen and found nothing untoward.

"Look what I've found at the bottom of a drawer."

Lucy sat on the bed and took the album from her and started going through the pages slowly. "Wow this is interesting. Well done Ellie. You were right to want to search."

Ellie looked puzzled. "It's only a photo album not the crown jewels. What's so exciting about it."

"Look here." Lucy pointed to a photo near the end.

Ellie looked and could see nothing out of place. It was of two men, arms around each other. They were looking in each other's eyes.

"Yeah so what."

"Look closely. One of them matches your description of Ashley. I would have said it was of two lovers."

"Lovers! But he had a girlfriend. He can't be gay."

"Can't he?"

Ellie took a closer look and saw exactly what Lucy was getting at. "Wow this changes everything. If Belinda knew of this it would give her the perfect motive for murder."

"Exactly," said Lucy, satisfied that Ellie had finally grasped the issue.

"I would also suggest Tammy doesn't know Ashley as well as she thought she did as she never mentioned a man friend."

"She could be hiding it from us. We know someone isn't telling the truth."

"You're right, but why hide it? There isn't a stigma attached to liking the same sex as there used to be."

"I'm not at all sure Tammy is as innocent as she makes out. Don't forget the skeleton which we have no explanation for. Something strange is going on there. She gives me the creeps actually."

"I'd never thought about it. The skeleton I find creepy but not her. I feel more sorry for her. She has no life to speak of and she is so young."

"It could be said that having no life means she has found rather macabre hobbies."

"What do you mean?" queried Ellie, feeling somewhat confused. She wasn't usually slow on the uptake but Lucy seemed a long way ahead of her.

"Well life must be very boring. She needs something to occupy her during those long hours spent resting."

Ellie continued to look puzzled much to Lucy's frustration. She felt she'd spelt it out well but her friend still wasn't grasping it.

"Are you being thick today?"

"I think I am," agreed Ellie, not at all put out by Lucy's insult.

"Look, she's at home with no visitors, or not that we know of. What does she do? She has to keep her mind active somehow. She has a skeleton and loads of paper stuck on the wall."

"So what?"

Lucy sighed, this really was hard work.

"I think she could have staged this with Ashley so she can have some excitement in her dull life."

"You what? If you are right, and I'm not sure I agree, what would Ashley get out of it by disappearing leaving blood in the bath. Also they would be in trouble for wasting police time if it got discovered. You're really not making any sense."

"I see your point. Maybe I did get a bit carried away for a minute there."

"A bit?! Very if you ask me."

"Ok. Pulling back a bit we still have this interesting photo. It means we should really speak to Belinda again or Tammy first to see what she knows about the situation. He may have confided in Tammy."

"I agree with you. I wouldn't know how to approach it though without letting on what we've found out as we don't know who to trust if anyone."

"What do you suggest we do then? Call the police and hand it over to them. Of course they would want to know how we got into the flat in the first place and why we were searching. We would get ourselves in trouble that we couldn't easily talk ourselves out of."

"I'm starting to wish I had never suggested searching his flat now."

"Just as I'm glad we did as it's taken us further forward. Come on we ought to continue to see what else we can find. We have been here too long already."

Ellie nodded and they put everything back as Ellie had found it before continuing searching.

In the living room they found a P45 in a drawer.

"Hey Lucy look at this."

"That's interesting. Do you think he had just lost his job or changed it."

"This changes everything. Maybe it was suicide."

"This proves we need to get more information out of Belinda and Tammy."

"But how? We can't ask anything without admitting that we've committed an offence to find this information. I wouldn't want to trust either of them."

"I know what you mean but I don't know how else we can do it. It needs to be approached carefully I admit, but as you know I don't do subtle."

"You think that's news. I know that of course. I should just hand you a sledgehammer as that's how you blurt everything out."

"Come on I think we should get going. We've already been here longer than we should have."

"You're getting twitchy."

"So should you be. Everyone knows no one is here at the moment so if they hear movement they might phone the police."

"All right, just let me take a photo of these possible clues so that we can refer to them as needed."

This done they quickly left the flat being careful to shut the door as quietly as possible.

Back in the flat Lucy breathed a sigh of relief. She collapsed on to the sofa and leaned back closing her eyes.

"Are you all right?" asked Ellie with some concern.

"Just waiting for my heart rate to settle down. It feels as if my heart is going to explode out of my chest any minute."

"I'll put the kettle on. Tea will soon sort us out."

"You don't seem bothered. You're keeping your cool."

"I have to. One of us needs to be on the ball just in case."

"In case of what?" asked Lucy getting into more of a panic as she imagined all sorts of horrors that could befall them.

"What if we were seen."

"Don't say that." The look of fear that crossed Lucy's face was too much for Ellie who immediately felt contrite.

"I'm sure no one did so don't look so worried. They would have confronted us or called the police."

"Now you've planted the idea in my mind I can't just remove it."

"I'm sorry, I should have kept my mouth shut. I wasn't thinking what a delicate little flower you were."

"I'm not usually. I don't know what's come over me, I really don't."

"Neither do I. Anyway I'd better go and put the kettle on for that tea I promised you."

Ellie went across the room to the kitchen where she prepared the tea. Her mind was elsewhere thinking what she had found when her phone rang. Lucy went and passed it to her as Ellie hadn't heard it, so far away she was in her mind.

"Hello Tammy…..yes this afternoon would be good…bye."

"That was Tammy," stated Ellie.

"I realised that," said Lucy drily. "I hope she didn't know we were searching Ashley's flat and that's what she wants to speak to us about."

"I doubt it," said Ellie. "She probably wants the company that's all."

"She never just wants company. It's always connected to the case."

"Very true. If it worries you that much you could stay here. I'll make your apologies."

"And be left on tenterhooks, no thanks. I'm coming with you. We are the detective duo after all. You don't do anything without me."

Ellie smiled. She knew Lucy wouldn't want to be left out of the story, hearing it only second hand from Ellie. Theirs was a true partnership, doing everything together. Just like the three musketeers whatever their names were. Ellie couldn't think off the top of her head. She would trust Lucy with her life.

Lucy sipped her tea in the quietness and started to relax slightly. Ellie noticing this was pleased, although she said nothing, that would only put Lucy's back up. It was the sort of things that didn't pop up in the middle of a sermon, not that either of them knew this not being church goers.

Chapter Ten

"How are you getting on?" asked Tammy.

"What do you mean?" queried Lucy, hoping not to blush and give away what they had been up to in Ashley's flat. She hated this about herself but she went red over nothing.

"Ashley of course. I know you are investigating his disappearance," said Tammy.

"How did you know?" asked Ellie.

"It's obvious as we've spoken before about him and you've asked a lot of questions."

"True. We're not getting far actually. We don't know anyone involved in his life, his work. Belinda insists she's been dumped by Ashley some time ago."

Tammy was surprised. "I'm sure Ashley would have told me if that were the case. But it gives her a motive doesn't it."

"Does it?"

"Of course. She's obviously a jealous lover and killed him thinking if she can't have him then no one else can."

"We hadn't thought of that," said Lucy.

"Even more so if she knows who his new partner is."

"He's got a new partner?" queried Ellie, not daring to look at Lucy. They were certainly finding out more here. It raised questions in her mind though. Why was Tammy being so helpful suddenly when previously stating she knew nothing. Had she been in communication with Ashley all the time? Ellie found herself being highly suspicious of Tammy and her motives. It could also be the other way around and Tammy was making things up to put them off the scent. How she longed to discuss the situation with Lucy.

"I've seen him leaving the building with a man, arm in arm," said Tammy.

At this Ellie and Lucy looked at each other. What was making Tammy so cooperative?

"That could mean anything. They could just be friends," said Lucy.

"No, it must be more than that," said Tammy. "The way they were gazing into each others eyes."

"Why suddenly tell us now when you've insisted you know nothing more than what you'd already told us?" blurted out Lucy, stopping abruptly when she saw

Ellie shaking her head slightly. Lucy realised she had let her mouth speak without thinking again. One of these days she would get them both into trouble.

Tammy was silent. Clearly not wanting to answer that question. In fact she finished the remains of her tea and stood up saying she needed a rest. Ellie and Lucy stood up also and left Tammy.

Back in Ellie's flat she turned to Lucy saying, "When will you learn to keep your mouth shut? We finally seemed to be getting somewhere then you had to put your foot in your mouth again."

"I know," sighed Lucy. "For what it's worth I'm sorry. I knew what I'd done as soon as I said it. I just hope we haven't lost her cooperation completely."

"So do I," said Ellie not about to let Lucy off the hook so easily. The two fell into an uneasy silence, neither knowing what to say. Ellie still felt exasperated with Lucy and her big mouth and Lucy felt horribly guilty.

…………

It was a few hours later when it was pitch black outside that Ellie spoke, "I'm sorry for what I said to you. I know you well and know what you're like. Maybe I could have interrupted to stop you instead of leaving you to be your usual subtle self."

"You don't need to apologise. I deserved it. I really need to learn."

"You'll never learn now. If you were going to you would have done so years ago."

"Are you hinting that I'm too old to change?" asked Lucy, a dangerous tone in her voice.

"No I didn't say that."

"I know you didn't. You could have been subtly suggesting it though to rub my nose in it."

"Now would I do that?" asked Ellie.

"Yes," said Lucy.

"Well if that's what you think."

"I do, but you better watch out as I'll get my own back. You're the same age as me don't forget."

"I'm frightened," said Ellie pretending to shiver.

"Haha, very funny."

"I thought so," said Ellie. The two women laughed together which completely dissipated the tension that had been there between them. That was something enviable about their friendship. They would argue and fall out but never for very long. In fact it wasn't often that it happened.

"Anyway, we've found out from Tammy that Ashley was seeing a man, so it's likely that Belinda knew that too which gives her motive."

"Motive for what? We don't even know there's a problem yet."

"I suppose I'm thinking more now that he was murdered."

"I really want to look at his work records and speak to his colleagues. That would give us more to go on. Maybe he's even seeing someone from work that he's met."

"I'm sure Tammy must know about that really or she doesn't know him well or not as much as she claims. Also, Belinda would know as an ex girlfriend."

"I don't know how to find out though. To ask questions will be obvious that's what we're trying to do which could be a disaster considering both of them could be suspects. We don't want to find ourselves targeted by a murderer."

"Potential murderer I think you mean."

"I stand corrected!" said Ellie. "But Tammy does have that skeleton which is so macabre."

"There is something else on my mind as well. I can't believe we didn't think about sooner but didn't you realise there was no blood in the bath?"

"You're right it didn't register with me. It just looked as you'd expect it to look."

There was silence as the two women were lost in thought for some time. It was left to Ellie to break it by saying, "The police wouldn't have cleaned it as it's evidence. Either the perpetrator must have done it or Ashley himself has been back. It makes it more suspicious that foul play was involved."

"I agree," said Lucy. "We can be fairly certain it isn't Ashley so there must be someone else involved."

"This is doing my head in. Why don't we watch the news before visiting Mick?"

Lucy reached for the remote control and passed it to Ellie who put the television on.

"A body of an adult male has been found in the Blackbeard Park. Police investigating think it could be linked to the recent disappearance of a man in the local area."

Ellie and Lucy looked at each other and Lucy began, "You don't think….."

Ellie cut in, "That's what I'm thinking as well."

If the body had turned up it changed everything. If it could be identified as Ashley then they would know it was murder. It might not make their investigation any easier, in fact it would make it worse as the police would be sniffing round asking more questions and Belinda and Tammy were less likely to talk about it.

Ellie's phone rang, "Hello Tammy…yes we were just watching it and saw…that's what we think as well. Sorry we can't come now as we were just leaving to visit Lucy's husband in hospital. We can drop round tomorrow after work if that's any help…ok see you then."

"Well?" asked Lucy. "What did she want?"

"Give me a chance I've just disconnected the call," said Ellie before continuing. "She sounded as if it was urgent she speak to us before the police get round here. I even thought she wanted to cooperate now."

"Could it be we're getting somewhere maybe?"

"I'm not holding my breath on that one. I think we might if we approach it carefully," said Ellie. "Meantime if we don't move we'll miss visiting time and you won't be happy about that."

"You're right. We should get going."

They put the mystery to one side and concentrated their thoughts on Mick throughout the journey to the hospital.

………

Mick wasn't fooled, he noticed straight away that the two women were distracted by something and guessed it must be the mystery. Lucy quickly filled him in on the latest.

"I really think you should leave it to the police if it is Ashley who's been found. It could be dangerous and you don't know enough about his life to investigate and speak to the right people anyway."

"We solved the murder of Phyllis remember so we're quite capable of solving this one," said Ellie.

"Ok, ok," said Mick calmly. "I wasn't trying to offend you. This is different however, as you don't know the victim or anything about his life. His ex girlfriend won't talk to you and what has been said could be lies, the same with Tammy. I appreciate your good intentions but this one isn't for you."

Lucy looked downcast as she took in what her husband was saying. She knew what he said was true but didn't want to admit to it. She actually enjoyed investigating mysteries and she suspected her friend felt the same. She glanced at Ellie and saw a mutinous look on her face.

Mick said, "I can see you're going to ignore me as usual, just try and stay out of trouble with the police and with the suspects."

"We will," said Lucy smiling before leaning over to kiss her husband. "Thanks darling. You're one in a million."

"I have to be to cope with you and your friend and all the antics you get up to. You two are a liability. You shouldn't be let loose on the public on your own or even together. In fact it's worse when the two of you are as one."

Lucy again leaned over to kiss her husband whom she adored. She knew she and Ellie had his full support whatever he may be saying. He was the common sense part of the trio who liked to keep the women grounded. There was no telling what would happen if he didn't step in at times.

Ellie sat quietly watching the interaction between the couple. She felt a twinge of jealousy that she didn't have the same. She was alone now since her husband was sent to prison for domestic violence. Lucy and Mick did try and include her in their plans but it wasn't the same, she still felt like a spare part.

"Are you all right?" Mick asked Ellie. "You're very quiet."

Ellie nodded, "Yes, I'm fine. Just watching you two lovebirds."

"Well we have to make up for lost time. We don't see each other so much whilst I'm stuck in this place. I can't wait to get out of here. I'm starting to go stir crazy sitting here with the occasional slow walk down the ward and back."

"If we could break you out we would. You're better off here though until they feel you're ready to go home. They know what they're doing."

"I know," sighed Mick.

Chapter Eleven

Ellie and Lucy were sipping their tea with Tammy who was clearly having a bad day, laying on the sofa. Her lips were set in a straight line indicating that she was in a lot of pain.

"Are you sure you want to speak to us? You don't seem well at all," enquired Lucy.

"It's ok…..I think I'll manage…..I didn't sleep much last night."

"I take it you saw the news about the body in the park," stated Ellie.

Tammy nodded, relieved at not having to answer. She was feeling a lot worse than she was letting on. The reality was she wasn't well enough to see anyone but she wanted to get this over and done with. She was sure the body was that of Ashley and wanted to tell Ellie and Lucy everything she knew. It was time to be completely open with them. She had guessed some time back that the two friends were trying to investigate Ashley's disappearance. She didn't know why but wasn't sure she really cared, as long as the perpetrator was brought to justice it was fine by her.

"The body….I'm sure it's Ashley. He had….told me he was…..going to stay with friends for a while. He was…frightened."

"Did he say what or who was scaring him?" asked Lucy.

Tammy shook her head. "It was the tone of his voice….that made….me think that."

"Did you ask?" asked Ellie.

Tammy again shook her head. "I was….having a bad….day and just couldn't. I regret…it now. Until the news….I really thought….that was…where he was."

"Did Belinda know this?" asked Lucy.

"I don't know. I hadn't seen….Belinda around for a while actually."

"How was he able to take time off work to be with friends."

Tammy shrugged, then grimaced as pain shot down her arms. "I just….assumed he was….taking holiday."

"You really don't seem well," said Lucy. "I'm not sure we should be staying and encouraging you to talk. We don't want to make you feel worse because you're overdoing it instead of resting."

"I want to….get this done….so you can investigate…..knowing everything I do."

"How did you know we were investigating anything?" asked Ellie out of genuine curiosity.

"It's obvious….because….of all….the questions….you've been trying…..to…ask."

"You're really not fit for this at the moment. You can barely talk."

"It's an effort," admitted Tammy feeling too ill to pretend otherwise.

"One thing before we go that we would like to clear up," said Lucy. "What is that skeleton doing in your room?" Ellie was looking daggers at her friend but Lucy was keen to have an answer to clear up that mystery.

"It's innocent honestly."

"It doesn't look it," said Lucy as blunt as usual.

"You don't have to answer if you don't want to."

"I really should explain myself.....but I can't....at the moment."

"We understand, don't we Lucy," Ellie said, looking meaningfully at her friend.

Lucy nodded, not daring to say anything else in case she incurred more of Ellie's wrath.

....

"What possessed you. You knew she wasn't feeling well and not up to explaining anything yet you still had to go and ask."

"I know. It's my mouth running away with me again."

"That question could have waited especially as it was obvious Tammy wanted to be open and honest with us."

"I know," sighed Lucy. "Curiosity got the better of me and I didn't think."

Ellie shook her head, despairing of her friend. "It's done now, let's forget it. She'll give us the answer when she's feeling better."

"Do you really think she's that ill."

"Yes of course. She looked terrible you only had to look at her."

"It's just ME has such a bad press you have to wonder."

"No you don't. It's obvious it's real and very severe. You only have to look at Tammy to know that. What's wrong with you anyway. It's not like you to doubt people."

"I dunno. Maybe it's that skeleton that creeps me out."

"That has nothing to do with how ill she is or even if she's ill to start with."

"I agree. I don't know what got into me."

"You're not the person I know that's for sure."

"Maybe it's Mick being so ill in hospital. He's never far from my mind. I came so close to losing him that….." Lucy stopped abruptly unable to continue. Her eyes shone with unshed tears.

Ellie reached over and put her arm around her friend. "I know," she said. "He's on the mend now so you should be able to relax."

Lucy nodded before saying, "It's seeing how close it was that reminded how frail our hold on life really is. I thought of Tammy dying before we got the answers we need."

"You're right. I do understand what you're saying and how you came to blurt it out."

Lucy cheered up slightly at this. "Why don't we go out for a meal instead of coming back and cooking after visiting Mick."

"That's a good idea. Where shall we go."

"Why don't we go to that new Chinese restaurant that's just opened up."

"Ok that should give us a laugh trying to eat with chopsticks."

"You can if you want but I'm using a knife and fork as usual."

"You can't do that. We have to eat as the natives do if we go to their restaurant."

"I know I haven't a hope if I use chopsticks."

"Nor have I but we still have to give it a try."

Lucy said nothing. She knew neither of them would succeed with the sticks. She didn't know how anyone managed it. She had never got the hang of it at all. Too much like hard work and she wanted her food while it was hot not lukewarm or even cold while failing miserably with the sticks.

....

Mick couldn't help noticing how downcast his wife looked as she and Ellie walked down the ward towards him. Well he had some good news that would cheer her up.

"Guess what?" said Mick before the two friends had even had a chance to sit down.

"Let us sit down first can't you."

"Sorry I'm so excited."

Lucy catching on before he said anything further asked, "When?"

"Monday after I've seen the doctor."

Lucy's eyes shone and a genuine smile lit up her face. She forgot what had occurred previously with Tammy. Her thoughts were just on getting her husband home with her.

"I'll have to be careful not to overdo anything though," warned Mick.

"That's all right I won't let you lift a finger. You'll be the most spoiled husband in the world."

"Why thank you slave."

"Hey, I didn't say I would be your slave did I. In fact I don't even remember mentioning the word."

"You didn't, I did," said Mick with a cheeky grin on his face.

Ellie watched the exchange going on between the lovebirds. She was really pleased for them but wondered what it would mean for their investigation as Lucy would no longer be sharing the flat. They won't be together to talk it through and didn't want to crowd Lucy with thoughts as all her time would be taken up looking after her husband.

Mick noticed and guessed what she was thinking. "Don't worry, you can still come round to discuss your latest case. Maybe I'll be able to point you in the right direction."

"I wouldn't want to intrude, and anyway you'll need your rest."

"Don't be silly. Besides it's my heart that's a bit dodgy not my brains. I can still use that you know."

"I stand corrected," said Ellie.

Visiting time flew by and it wasn't long before the bell was going to signal time was up. The ward sister saw Lucy with a big grin on her face and spoke to her. "You must be pleased to get him home again. But don't forget he has to take things easy for the time being. We don't want to see him back here again."

"He won't I can assure you. We've already agreed I'll be his willing slave."

"Good," said the sister approvingly.

The two friends left the ward and walked to the car. They hadn't been able to park in the hospital car park. They'd left the car in a small side road.

"I'm so pleased for you," said Ellie.

"I can't wait. I'd better spend tomorrow at the house sorting everything out. I'll make up a bed on the sofa so he doesn't have to climb stairs. I must clean the place from top to bottom as well."

"I'll come and help."

"You don't have to."

"Of course I do. We're friends aren't we? It will be a pleasure to help get everything ready."

"The detective duo will have to be on hold."

"Not for long though. As Mick said it's not a problem with his brains. He's happy to think through what we tell him. I for one would love to have his opinion and suggestions for the way forward."

"I'm not sure I'll let him get involved."

"You can't wrap him in cotton wool completely. It will give him something to do in the long hours he'll spend on his own."

Lucy looked startled. "He won't be on his own. I'll be with him."

"What about work?"

"I'll take time off of course."

"Have you got holiday owing. It's the end of the tax year coming up."

"I'm going to try and get it as compassionate leave as well as holiday."

"That's a thought. I didn't think of that."

"That's because I'm the brains of the detective duo."

"I'll have you know I have perfectly good brains," said Ellie in a hoity toity voice.

"Oh yeah?"

The two women burst out laughing before Ellie had a chance to say anything further. They could always find something to laugh at however dire the circumstances. Their colleagues envied them their close friendship and their ability to laugh in the midst of trouble and chaos, although some felt it to be inappropriate. Ellie and Lucy didn't care what others thought. It was how they dealt with life. They had been known to comment, "If you can't see the funny side you'd be miserable all the time."

Chapter Twelve

"Is Lucy not with you?" asked Tammy.

Ellie shook her head. "Her husband's out of hospital now so she's gone back home. She's off work for a couple of weeks to look after him."

"You must miss her, you're both so close."

"I do. I always saw her at work and quite often we'd spend the evening together, but I've been giving them some space this week. Lucy said it was all right but it didn't feel ok if you know what I mean."

"I understand, although I've never had a close friendship like the two of you share."

"Anyway, before you get too tired we better go back to the conversation we were having last time we were here."

"When I explain about the skeleton and all the paper. Well, I have always been interested in crime drama on television especially in the forensics and one day I was rummaging at a car boot sale when I saw it. It was gorgeous and I knew I had to have it. It's lived in my bedroom ever since. All the paper well, that's because I like to follow real cases and see if I can solve the murders."

"So that's why you had so much details about Ashley?" asked Ellie relieved. This explained so much providing Tammy was telling the truth and she felt instinctively that she was.

"Exactly. The problem is I can't go out and question anyone. I decided I needed to make friends with you and allow you to investigate for me."

"Wait a minute, I'm a bit confused. You seem to have lied to us about Belinda and Ashley's relationship and one of you lied about his parents. There were too many contradictions in the story."

"I know and I'm sorry about that. I didn't know if I could trust you or not."

"You've just done it again. You say you wanted us to investigate but you didn't trust us so you lied. How were we supposed to get anywhere?"

"I'm sorry," said Tammy, reddening. "From now on you'll get the truth honest."

"How can we trust you. For all we know you could be the murderer."

"How when I can't get out and I'm not physically strong enough to do anything."

"That's something we don't know, but you can see where I am coming from."

"I suppose so. Look I'm really sorry. I'll understand if you don't want to know the information I have."

"I didn't say that. I'll listen but when I tell Lucy we'll weigh it up to see if it could be the truth or not."

"I suppose I'll have to accept that. I know I deserve it."

Ellie nodded and said, "You'll have to earn our trust."

"Ashley and Belinda had broken up just as she told you. It was Ashley who dumped Belinda. She wasn't happy and kept on turning up here for a week or so. I saw her out of my window. I warned Ashley to be careful because I was worried about how far Belinda would take this stalking business."

"You really felt she might be a threat?"

Tammy nodded. "It was the look on her face. I dunno, I can't describe it."

"Ok."

"What made you suspect it could be murder? Obviously you didn't see the blood in the bath."

"He was going to stay with friends he said. He was scared of something although he didn't say what. I just assumed it might be something to do with Belinda."

"Was she still coming round?"

Tammy shook her head.

"What made you think it had something to do with Belinda then?"

"Because there was something about her I didn't like. I never could see what Ashley saw in her."

"Was he seeing anyone else?"

"He hadn't said but I suspected he was."

"So you don't know them then?"

Tammy shook her head. "I think it was a man."

"What makes you say that?" Ellie was being very careful not to lead Tammy down a path in case Tammy didn't know anything and just agreed because she wanted to feel useful.

"I saw them together once and it was the way Ashley glanced at him. There was a hungry look in his eyes."

"What do you mean? You make it sound like he wanted to ravage him"

"That's exactly how it was."

Ellie wasn't sure what to make of this. Ok, she had seen the photo but what Tammy was saying sounded a bit extreme. Could she be imagining it? Ellie made a mental note to discuss it with Lucy when she saw her next.

Ellie decided to take a risk and said, "What about the man that was running away the day it all started?"

"It could have been his lover I suppose."

"Had you ever seen them coming in and out together."

"No," admitted Tammy.

"Yet you still think they were lovers?"

"Definitely."

"Where were they getting together if it wasn't here?"

"That I don't know."

"Did you ever speak to Ashley about this man?"

"I tried but he never responded, just said he was with Belinda, until they broke up that is."

"Could he have been frightened of this man?"

"Never," said Tammy looking surprised. "If you had seen the love and adoration in his eyes you would understand what I'm trying to say."

"Ok."

The two women sat in silence for some time, neither one sure what needed to be said next. Ellie's mind was whizzing at a million miles an hour trying to digest everything she had learned.

"Could you clear up one mystery that's bugging me?"

"I will if I can," responded Tammy, wanting to be helpful.

"It's about Ashley's parents. You claim they are dead but Belinda says the opposite and says Ashley goes there a lot. She thought that was the most likely place for him to have disappeared to."

"I can only tell you what Ashley told me. He told me they died many years ago in an accident. They were on a skiing holiday. They were out when the weather turned nasty. It was a real blizzard Ashley said. They didn't stand a chance. They went off the run and fell down the mountain."

"Where was Ashley?"

"He was staying with grandparents. He only knew what he was told. He was ten at the time."

Ellie was silent. How tragic that was for such a young child.

Tammy interrupted her thoughts, "He remained living with them until eighteen when he went to university. His grandparents died in a car accident while he was in his final year. It really messed up his exams he said."

"Interesting that his family all died in accidents."

"I'd never thought any more about it. I just accepted what Ashley told me."

"Hmm," murmured Ellie. She wasn't sure what to think of the latest. There was certainly a contradiction when previously she had said he was in foster care. Was it just a coincidence or was Ashley lying. He could be trying to get sympathy or could he have been involved in their deaths in some way. She wasn't sure how at that moment, but she would certainly be discussing the situation with Lucy and Mick. This was definitely where she would value input from Mick. He could be relied on for the common sense approach.

Ellie glanced at her watch. "I really should get going now. Is there anything further you can think of that I should know."

Tammy sat lost in thought for a minute before shaking her head, "I don't think so."

"Ok, we'll leave it there for now. We can always have another chat at a later date if I think of anything else."

"Thank you for listening and taking me seriously," said Tammy standing up to see Ellie to the door.

"It's ok I can see myself out. You rest. You must be worn out by now."

"I am rather," admitted Tammy. "I think I'll have a lie down now."

"Enjoy your rest."

"I won't. It's a pain in the neck having to rest so much. I can't get anything done because any time I start something it's soon time to go back to bed again. I'm sick of the sight of bed. If I ever get better I'll never lie in bed again."

"I understand where you are coming from as it must be frustrating and boring for you but bed is nice at the appropriate time."

"I know what you mean, but if you had been like this for as long as I have you would feel the same way."

"I probably would," agreed Ellie.

Chapter Thirteen

Ellie was just walking in the door when her phone rang. She dropped her key and quickly routed in her bag for her phone. She was always losing it into the bottomless pit that was her bag. She swore it was like the Bermuda Triangle! Finding it she took the call. Before she had time to say anything Lucy's voice cut in sounding frenzied.

"Did you hear the news? They identified the body as Ashley."

"Oh gosh. So it's real then, we are dealing with murder."

"You didn't hear it?"

"No, I've just walked in from seeing Tammy."

"I forgot you were seeing her today."

"You're definitely not with it, but you haven't been since Mick came out of hospital."

"I know. I think I'm going to have to tie him to the chair sometimes. He's driving me mad as he wants to do everything. He says he's sick and tired of resting."

"I can understand that. Tammy was saying she feels the same."

"It must be worse for her because she's been like it for so long and doesn't know when or if it will ever end. At least with Mick we know he will recover he just has to take it easy."

"Look do you want me to fill you in on my conversation with Tammy? It was quite enlightening."

"Why don't you come over and we can discuss it with Mick as well."

"Are you sure?"

"Absolutely certain. It might help if Mick has something to occupy his mind. Stop him from getting bored and driving me to distraction."

"Okay dokey, on my way. See you soon."

Ellie dropped her phone back in her bag and picked up the keys which were on the floor at her feet. At least she didn't have to hunt for them. She rushed out and decided to drop in on Tammy briefly to tell her the news. She thought her new friend would want to know the latest.

Tammy was white faced when she opened the door. She looked in surprise at Ellie and said, "You've only just left. Did you leave something behind?"

Ellie shook her head and told her the news about Ashley. Tammy's eyes filled with tears. Although she had guessed her friend was dead she still wasn't prepared to hear it.

"Will you be all right?" asked Ellie with some concern. "I was on my way to see Lucy and Mick. We're going to discuss the situation and see where we go from here, but if you need me I could stay for a bit."

"I wish I could go with you," sighed Tammy.

"I know. You need to rest though. You look terrible. I wouldn't have stayed so long if I had realised how much it would wipe you out."

Tammy nodded and said, "I need to lie down before I fall down. I'm feeling rather faint suddenly."

"I'll help you," said Ellie putting her bag down just inside the door and going in. She put her arm around Tammy to offer some support and walked slowly with her to her bedroom and on to the bed. Tammy sighed with relief.

"That skeleton doesn't look so bad now I know the truth about how you acquired it."

"Good. It was never my intention to frighten anyone. It didn't even occur to me that it might be viewed as suspicious."

"Have you got a name for it?"

"Yes, I call it Bernie."

"An interesting name."

"It was the first name that came into my head," said Tammy, although there was a queer look crossed her face which wasn't lost on Ellie.

There was something about the name which Tammy wasn't saying. There was still a mystery here somewhere.

Ellie had a strange feeling that Tammy was involved somehow or knew more than she was letting on about Ashley's death. There was something about the name Bernie as well. If she were right Tammy knew someone with that name, but were they alive or dead! This brought her back to the immediate problem of Ashley. Had Tammy told her everything, or most of it. Was she a reliable source of information? After all, she had lied before so there was no guarantee she hadn't done so again. She couldn't wait to discuss everything including her current thoughts with Lucy and Mick.

....

"You took your time," said Lucy as she let her friend in.

"I thought I'd drop by Tammy's and let her know the latest news then I helped her back to bed as she looked terrible and admitted to feeling faint. We then had another conversation about the skeleton."

"Let me make you a cup of tea then you can tell us all about it. You can entertain Mick whilst I put the kettle on."

Ellie, who would rather have started chatting with Lucy went reluctantly to say hello to Mick in the living room.

"She's putting the kettle on is she?" queried Mick.

Ellie nodded as she sat down. "How are you?" she asked.

"I feel fine, just fed up at having to rest so much."

"You don't want another heart attack do you. Don't you find you get tired quickly?"

Mick nodded and admitted it was so. He still hated it though. His body kept betraying him. He knew deep down he wasn't up to much as yet.

"How's work?" he asked, desperately casting round for conversation which wouldn't involve his health. He was quite fed up with Lucy asking at what seemed like every minute how he was. He needed stimulation and he hoped his wife's friend would provide it.

"Work's fine I suppose. It's not much fun without Lucy though. Her presence was enough to enlighten any boring or difficult day."

"I know but she'll be back soon. I'll make sure she is, even if it's only part time hours at first."

"You're not talking about me going back to work are you," said Lucy coming through with a tray of tea for the three of them.

Mick nodded causing Lucy to say, "I've made it quite clear I'm not going back until you are firmly on the mend and ok to be left. At present it isn't going to happen. How do you think you'll get yourself a drink?"

"You could leave me a flask of tea, it's not a strenuous job pouring it out. You could also leave me a sandwich for lunch. All I'll have to do is get up for the toilet and that's all I'm doing now anyway."

"I'll think about it."

Mick had to be satisfied with that.

They sat in companionable silence while they sipped the hot tea. Ellie was eager to talk about her conversation with Tammy before and after the news of Ashley's death reached her.

Lucy could see the restlessness in her friend and took pity on her. "Come on then, I can see you're dying to give us the latest information. You've obviously found out quite a bit to be so on edge."

Ellie nodded and told her two friends about her latest chats with Tammy.

"Wow!" exclaimed Lucy. "You've certainly picked up a lot there but it doesn't tell us where to go from here.

"I was thinking we need to speak to Belinda again. See what we can get out of her in the light of new evidence."

"Do you think it's worth it? She was very reluctant to talk last time."

"I think it's worth a try," said Mick butting in on the conversation. "You might find she wants to be more cooperative knowing that Ashley is dead and not staying with his parents or anyone else. You could also try showing that you can call her out on the lies she has told. You might be able to ascertain the truth of Tammy's statement. After all, we can't be sure Tammy is telling the truth based on recent evidence to the contrary. You can ask for details of Ashley's parents from Belinda. You could at least verify who is telling the truth."

Ellie nodded, "That's what I was thinking. I don't see how we can approach his parents if we work on the assumption they are alive. Why would they talk to us. They would be in contact with the police but they don't know us. We're just two ordinary podiatrists."

"Great minds think alike," said Lucy, not at all jealous of Ellie. She knew she and Mick were a solid couple. Besides she knew Ellie was wary of men after being so badly treated by her soon to be ex, Simon. "I agree I don't think we can contact his parents."

"You don't have to. Just a phone call to them and confirm they are who Belinda claims them to be."

"I didn't keep a note of Belinda's contact details so I'll have to ask Tammy. I just hope Belinda will agree to meet with us again."

"It's a pity we can't arrange it now," said Lucy who wasn't exactly patient.

She was always rushing at everything and wanted things done that very minute. She never took on students or newly qualified podiatrists at work because she would easily lose her cool with them. She had no time for mistakes. Ellie had to admit that the podiatrists who were coming as their first job were not up to much although she didn't know why. Presumably they got the same training as she and Lucy had received in the dim and distant past, but all the evidence pointed to the contrary. It was worrying the state the profession was in. Those who were old school were fast approaching retirement age and then what? People's feet could be left to rot under the care of those just entering the profession.

Ellie tried not to dwell on this. There was nothing she could do about it and anyway they were supposed to be concentrating on the more immediate problem at hand. If she didn't bring her thoughts back to the present she could see that they would soon end up reminiscing about the past – and that covered decades of conversation, the good and the bad. She didn't regret anything. She loved her job and she knew Lucy did as well. Times were changing though that was obvious. More recently she had begun thinking about retiring but with her split from Simon it wasn't an option, she needed the money. She also knew Lucy felt the same way as they had discussed it more than once. It appeared they would retire at the same time which wouldn't surprise any of their colleagues who were used to the terrible duo. It was like having a Siamese twin – joined at the hip.

Chapter Fourteen

"Tammy we really need to contact Belinda again. Can you give us her details please?" asked Ellie.

"I'm not sure I should."

"Why this turn around? You were all too happy to cooperate yesterday. Surely knowing Ashley is dead will have you wanting to know who did it and see the murderer brought to justice."

"It's just…."

"Just what exactly?"

"Nothing."

Ellie sighed. She was getting nowhere. She couldn't understand what had changed. It wasn't just a lack of cooperation it was also hostility she was sensing. Something had happened to change Tammy's mind and she wished she could find out what it was.

"Can you not give me anything? You must know what Ashley did for a living for example. It would be good to speak to his employers."

Tammy shook her head. "Sorry I can't get involved further."

"But you're not. You're just answering a few background questions we have."

"No sorry. I'd like you to leave now please."

Ellie saw nothing for it but to do as requested. To try any further would just push Tammy away even more. She needed to speak to Lucy and Mick urgently. Deciding to pop in and see them she went out to her car instead of going up to her flat. She didn't need to ring as she knew they would be in.

"Hello Ellie, we weren't expecting you tonight. You were going to pop into Tammy and come tomorrow," said Lucy in some surprise when she opened the door.

"Can I come in. I've spoken to Tammy and I've got no idea where we go from here. It's somewhat of a dead end."

"I take it you got nowhere when you contacted Belinda?" queried Mick from his place laying on the sofa.

"Hello Mick. I haven't been able to speak to Belinda. Tammy refused to cooperate and wouldn't give me her details. She wouldn't even give me any details of Ashley's employment."

"That's odd," said Lucy.

"That's what I thought. I couldn't push it either as she asked me to leave. She seemed hostile towards me in fact."

"How strange. She always seems so pleased to see us when I've been with you. She wants friends and I thought we were starting to become that to her."

"So did I, but it appears not."

"Something must have changed and pretty dramatically," said Mike.

"But what?"

"We'll probably never know," said Lucy feeling somewhat defeated.

"You're not giving up that easily are you?" asked Mick surprised. "It's not like you darling."

"I know but what can we do except leave it to the police to investigate."

"No, you're not doing that. We'll sort this out together. We need to think about what has changed Tammy. If we can come up with the answer we might just be able to persuade her otherwise."

"You don't think….no, it can't be that surely," said Ellie.

"What?" asked Mick.

"It's going to sound stupid."

"I doubt it. We need to think of everything and try to whittle it down from there. Go and get a notebook darling," said Mick turning to Lucy with the last request.

"We're just wasting our time," said Lucy, getting up anyway.

Mick was ready to take notes. "Go on Ellie what was it you were thinking?"

"It's going to sound strange but I was wondering if someone threatened her."

"That's not odd at all," said Mick. "In fact it goes along with my line of thinking."

"But who would threaten her?" asked Lucy, somewhat sceptical of this line of questioning.

"Anyone. Ashley's contacts probably know of Tammy's circumstances and know she's in all the time. They may think she could have seen something. Maybe removal of the body for example. After all someone got rid of the body as it seems likely he was killed in his flat, probably in the bath as that is where the blood was."

"I hadn't thought of that," said Lucy, starting to get interested again.

"Ah, you want to know now. A minute ago you thought we were on a pointless exercise."

"That was before you explained the thought and I can see it makes sense. It can only be the situation you outlined."

"You didn't think of it because right from the start there has been a question mark over Tammy's own innocence especially when the skeleton and papers with information were everywhere."

"But if you're right how do we go about reassuring Tammy and getting her to cooperate again?" asked Lucy.

"That I don't have an answer to at the moment," responded Mick. "We need to come up with a strategy. It will need to be a good one if we are to convince her to help us again."

"Why would that be a problem with Belinda though unless Belinda was the one scaring Tammy. If that were the case, then surely Tammy would feel able to give us Ashley's work details. This line of thought would also work vice versa."

"Clearly the situation is very complex. It would help if we knew of other important people in Ashley's life," said Mick.

"Why important people?" asked Lucy.

"You're not using your brain today," remarked Ellie. "That's if you've got one."

"What do you mean if I've got one. I've got a perfectly good one if you don't mind."

"That's what you think. You must have lost it or it's gone on holiday."

"Ok you two," said Mick, knowing what the two women were like when they got going. They could be at it all night and they would achieve nothing. "Answering your question Lucy, it's because it must be someone important. Any other person wouldn't bother with murder. Why would they? It would achieve nothing."

"Ok I see what you mean – or I think I do."

"At last," said Ellie.

"Are you still insinuating I don't have a brain?" asked Lucy with a hint of danger in her voice.

"Not now but I am suggesting you are slow."

Mick shook his head in despair. He'd known it was impossible getting them back to the topic in hand. He gave up and listened as the two continued back and forth until the laughter started.

"I've just had another thought," said Ellie when they had all calmed down again. "It must be a male because the footprint in the snow we decided was male."

"That only means it was a male who had just left the flat. It was probably a different person who committed the murder."

"I suppose so," said Ellie.

"Now who's not using their brain," said Lucy, keen to get her own back.

"Oh yeah. Just you wait….."

"I'm so scared," interrupted Lucy pretending to shake with fear.

"Ha ha, very funny," said Ellie. "I'll think up a nice slow torturous death for you."

"You wouldn't. You'd be lost without me around."

"Very true, but I'll get used to it."

"I don't think you would. Where would you get the laughs from. Who would lighten up staff meetings and training days if I wasn't around."

"You've got a point but since you're not going anywhere it doesn't matter and we're having a silly conversation."

"But just now you were plotting murder so I wouldn't be around would I."

"I didn't say when I was going to carry it out though did I?"

"I suppose not," commented Lucy.

"Ok ladies, can I bring you back to the matter in hand or we're never going to sort out this mess and decide where we go from here."

"I can see the only answer being….." Ellie stopped short. "What are you screwing your nose up and sticking your tongue out for?"

"Just getting my own back," said Lucy.

"Please you two. We're not going to achieve anything. What has put you two in this silly mood all of a sudden? When

Ellie arrived we were talking sensibly and now this. You've descended into chaos."

"Chaos? How?" asked Ellie.

"With your antics of course."

"You should be used to us by now," commented Lucy, looking tenderly at the husband she adored.

"I am that's why I'm trying to get you back to the present mystery and away from your silly war."

"Anyway, as I was saying before being distracted by Lucy," said Ellie pausing.

"Well, continue," said Mick.

"Sorry I can't remember what I was going to say. But I'm sure it was an important point."

Mick sighed with exasperation. They really needed to put their thinking caps on and be serious for a while.

Lucy said, "I think we need to go back to Tammy and point this out to her. It would be interesting to see her reaction."

"That's what I was going to say. How dare you steal my thunder?"

"How was I to know. You didn't say, in fact you said you couldn't remember. If you had said it first I wouldn't have repeated it would I."

Here we go again, Mick thought. He loved these two women with all his heart. There was never a dull moment with them around. He wouldn't change anything about them. Ellie was as dear to him as his wife.

"I'm getting tired now. I think I'll go to bed," said Mick, stopping the two women who had really got going again.

"Are you all right?" asked Lucy, a look of concern on her face.

"Yes, just tired. Listening to you two getting at each other has exhausted me."

Instantly the two women looked contrite and forgot their argument.

"I'll help you," said Lucy.

"I should go and leave you two lovebirds to get to bed," said Ellie standing up. "I'll pop in and see what I can get out of Tammy tomorrow."

"I think it would be better left a few days, give her time to think," said Mick sitting down again. "She might come to her senses during that time."

"Ok good idea," said Ellie.

Chapter Fifteen

"Hello can I come in Tammy?" asked Ellie.

"I'd rather you didn't. I have nothing further to add. Besides I need to rest."

"Ok, just quickly then can you tell me where Ashley worked. That's all I want to know."

"His job was in IT but he no longer worked for the company. He was busy looking for a job."

"Did he leave of his own free will."

A strange look came over Tammy's face which Ellie couldn't interpret. It was sort of furtive and hostile. Ellie started to think she had pushed her luck too far as she waited for Tammy to say something. That she hadn't shut the door on Ellie was surely a good sign.

"I'm not sure I should tell you anything else."

"You haven't given me anything yet. I don't know which company he worked for or if he parted on good terms. Don't you see it could be someone there who had the motive to kill him."

"I'm not sure if he knew anyone well enough to feel strongly about him."

"At least give me their details and I can make enquiries."

"I'd rather not."

"Why? It can't do any harm at this stage as he is already dead."

"But we're not."

Ellie found that a strange answer from Tammy and took it as evidence that she was indeed being threatened.

"Is the man you've seen Ashley with by any chance a work colleague?"

"It's possible but I don't know for sure as I was never introduced."

"So far we don't have much. We know Ashley was killed but that's about it. He had a girlfriend but they'd broken up and left him alone except for his work colleagues and this mystery man you mentioned. We don't know if his parents are alive or dead due to conflicting evidence. As things stand we are stuck unless you decide to cooperate again. You wanted us to look into this and find out who did it. You obviously have no faith in the police to find the correct culprit."

"Why should I trust you? You lived next door he could have spoken to you yet you claim to know nothing."

"What's going on here? You wanted to be friendly and now you are openly hostile and no longer seem to care who murdered your friend."

Tammy looked down at her feet but said nothing.

"Has someone said something and warned you off?"

"How did they know you were looking into it?"

"So I'm right someone has said something."

"I didn't say that," said Tammy.

"As good as," responded Ellie.

"He worked in IT at the paper company in Firbank and that's all I'm going to say."

"Thank you."

"I just hope I don't get into trouble for telling you that."

"You could always tell the police?"

Tammy's face took on a look of panic. "That would be even worse. At least you're at a disadvantage as you know nothing to start with."

"Who was it? Belinda?"

Tammy didn't answer.

"I'm assuming I'm right then. You're lack of response says it all. You do realise by not saying anything you could be shielding a murderer. She obviously has strong reasons for you to say nothing more so she must be involved somehow."

Tammy shrugged. "I know nothing."

"Well thanks for what you have said. It's something to go on at least."

"Be careful, I don't want to get into trouble. Life's hard enough without anything else added to it."

"Don't worry we'll be very careful how we approach this."

"What do you mean we? It can only be you. I can't risk anything getting out."

"It will just be Lucy and her husband Mick I tell. We are working together."

"I suppose," said a hesitant Tammy as she closed the door without even a goodbye.

Ellie felt dismissed at that rather abrupt response from Tammy. At least they now knew she was being threatened and it seemed most likely to be Belinda. But why? Unless of course it was Belinda who committed murder. Somehow Ellie doubted it as it would need a strong person to remove a dead man and place him in the park. In fact, he must have been kept hidden somewhere before being dumped in the park or he would have been found sooner. It was possible Belinda had help in dumping the body in which case they were looking for two people. No, somehow Ellie believed Belinda to be innocent. Just a heartbroken woman who had been in love with Ashley. At this thought Ellie started feeling sorry for the ex girlfriend even if she were guilty of threatening Tammy.

Another thought, what if Belinda knew a lot more than she was letting on and she was being threatened as well. Ellie shook her head, this was all getting somewhat complicated. She needed to talk to her friend and pick her brains and not leaving Mick out of the equation.

………

"Hi Lucy, I've just left Tammy and we have work information. He had lost his job as an IT consultant in Firbank."

"What about Belinda?"

"Nothing. I didn't even get over the threshold. I had to persuade Tammy to give me what she did. She reluctantly seemed to admit she has been threatened, but no idea who by. It seemed most likely to be Belinda from the conversation."

Ellie continued to relay the story to Lucy who was telling Mick as they went along.

"Why not put it directly on speaker phone?" asked Ellie.

"I didn't think of that."

"Stop being silly and do it now."

With speaker phone on Ellie repeated what she had already told Lucy.

"Hmm," said Mick.

"I agree Belinda must be behind the threats, but as you said Ellie it is unlikely she killed him. We need a lot more information about the job and why exactly he lost it. I'm sure that is what happened."

"I'll try and look up the company online and get as much information as I can, then tomorrow sometime I will contact them and see what information I can get."

"You do realise they may not talk to you as you're not police with access to warrants and other such awful things."

"I know," said Mick, "But you never know unless you try which is what I intend doing. I'll hopefully get to find out about what happened and if there were any disgruntled employees or any gossip they know about. I'll try and look on the internet tonight and first thing tomorrow I'll phone the company and turn on the charm. Why don't you come for dinner straight from work and I'll update you."

"That sounds a good plan."

"Wonderful," said Lucy. "I'll cook a nice lasagne for us."
"Yummy," said Ellie. "My favourite."
"I know."

Chapter Sixteen

Mick didn't find anything much on the company online. Nothing disturbing, suggesting they were in a financial mess so he was pretty sure that Ashley wasn't made redundant. Everything seemed above board. This left nothing for it but to ring them and see what they had to say – if anything. He wasn't convinced he would get much from them as it wasn't an official request for information. Mick wished he had been able to find something suspicious on the internet which might have given him some leverage. He would do his best though as he didn't want to disappoint the two women in his life. It would also give him something to do as he was bored and frustrated sitting around at home doing nothing but rest.

"Oh hello, I was wondering if you could put me through to human resources please," said Mick politely.

He still wasn't sure how he was going to play this but he needed to come up with something quickly.

"Good afternoon, Helen speaking. How may I help you?"

"Hello Helen. I'm ringing with a few questions about Ashley whom I believe recently left your company."

"Y…es," said Helen warily.

"What can you tell me about him and why he left?"

"Who are you?"

"I'm an interested person."

"Are you the police?"

"No. Why would you be expecting the police?"

"Well wasn't his body found recently?"

Mick didn't know how to respond. He was feeling as wary as Helen in how much he gave away.

"Have the police been in touch?"

"Well no, but...."

"I'm not sure I should say anything further."

"You haven't actually said anything yet," Mick pointed out.

Helen lowered her voice so that Mick had to strain to hear what she was saying. "Look I really shouldn't say anything but we were concerned about what he was actually doing with the figures."

"You don't mean fraud do you?"

"We...ll."

Mick guessed from the drawn out word that it could be but she wouldn't say anything further on the subject.

Taking a stab in the dark he said, "How about we meet somewhere tomorrow lunchtime?"

"I'm not sure if I should." Helen sounded very doubtful but Mick was determined and he felt with just a bit more pushing that Helen would agree.

They agreed on a time and place. Mick warned her he would have his wife with him but she was safe to talk to.

....

Lucy and Ellie arrived home to find Mick on edge. "Cor you two took your time didn't you. I was expecting you ages ago."

"We're the same time as usual," commented Lucy checking her watch.

"Sorry it's just I wanted to fill you in on what I've done today."

"Have you found some answers?" asked Ellie eagerly.

"Well no, not exactly. I did speak to someone in HR but she was reluctant to say anything over the phone. I arranged to meet up with her tomorrow to talk face to face which she agreed to. She did hint however that fraud may have been a possibility."

"Er, exactly how were you planning on meeting her? You're supposed to be resting remember," said Lucy.

Mick blushed, "I thought you'd take me."

"Oh you did. Tell me how I can be at work and with you at the same time."

"You could phone in sick," suggested Mick.

"How could you," said Lucy aghast at what she was hearing. "That would be as dishonest as you think Ashley may have been."

"I know but what else could I do? I wasn't getting anywhere over the phone and I could tell she wouldn't be happy to meet with just the two of you. Plus I made sure it was lunchtime so you could leave the building and get back to work in the afternoon."

"You've thought of everything."

"Yes," said Mick who was smiling now. He knew he'd got his way.

After enjoying the promised lasagne they sat down and tried to work out a strategy for approaching Helen. They hoped it wouldn't be necessary, that she would be more forthcoming away from the office especially as she had agreed to the meeting.

"Don't forget to see if there was anyone he seemed interested in, male or female. He may have met this man at work," said Ellie who had been quiet up until then.

"I had thought of that," said Mick.

"Maybe he wasn't romantically involved in anyone else. They could have been in on the fraud, if that's what it was."

"That's what I was thinking. Maybe he had cold feet and that's why he was killed. Maybe he threatened to go to the police."

"He might not have even been involved in it but happened to stumble across it somehow," said Ellie. "Do you think I should have another chat with Tammy to see what she says. She knows him better than anyone it seems."

"I wouldn't until we've heard what Helen had to say."

"I've had a sudden thought, do you think Helen could be involved herself and just wants to find out what we know before deciding if we are a threat?"

"I hadn't thought of that," admitted Mick.

"Me neither," said Lucy. "It's certainly something we should keep in mind."

"We don't know who to trust at the moment. We're being given so much contradictory information that we can't afford to trust anyone," said Ellie.

"Very true," said Mick and Lucy nodded in agreement.

"This is so complicated," complained Ellie. "At least last time we knew all the people involved and had some idea of what we were doing. This time we're going in blind. It's not surprising if people are suspicious of us as we are trying to get basic information which would have been known to us if we'd known Ashley."

"I know, but we can't give up now," said Mick. "I've got the bit between my teeth and I want to run with it."

"You mean it gives you something to do and to think about whilst being stuck here all day on your own," said Lucy, smiling fondly at her husband.

"You know me too well," said Mick beginning to laugh.

"I should do I've been married to you for long enough."

Ellie watched her friends and listened to their exchanges. She wished she had the love they obviously still shared for each other. If only Simon hadn't messed it up so badly. She shivered and hoped her friends wouldn't notice. They were too wrapped up in each other.

"Ok I think I'll go now," Ellie said, wanting to leave the two lovebirds to it.

"Ok, see you in the morning usual time. I'll drive this time since I have to go out at lunch time to meet Helen with Mick."

Chapter Seventeen

"Well do you think she'll even show up?" asked Lucy of Mick when they arrived at the agreed meeting place with Helen.

They were in a park which suited them. Open and public so if anything went wrong there would be witnesses. At least that was the idea but no one was around. Not even dog walkers had ventured out on a chilly, wet day.

Lucy shivered, "Brr, it's cold. Winter has still got an icy grip on us, even though it's been warmer of late."

"I know," responded Mick.

"There's someone approaching now," said Lucy turning to survey the park. "Do you think it's her?"

"I don't know. We'll just have to see what happens. She does seem to be approaching us though."

"Hello, are you Mick and Lucy," asked the stranger with some trepidation.

"Yes we are. You're Helen I presume," answered Mick.

Helen nodded and Mick held out his hand to shake in the truly British way.

"There's a bench over there shall we sit down," suggested Lucy.

With nods from the other two they wandered over to the bench and sat down.

"I hope you don't mind if I have my lunch at the same time," said Helen. "I don't have long and we're not allowed to eat at our desks."

In between mouthfuls Helen began to talk after looking around and seeing no one in sight. "I have to be careful to ensure we're not overheard. What I have to say must not be repeated. It might even be dangerous considering what happened to Ashley."

"You think his death might be linked to the fraud you hinted at over the phone?"

Helen nodded, chewing her ham sandwich.

"I've been looking over my shoulder ever since he disappeared wondering if I'll be next."

"Was it usual for Ashley to not turn up like that?"

"No. He was very conscientious about his job. He never missed a day. Even when others would go off sick he would turn up and struggle through the day. No one could persuade him to go home and return when he was better."

"What do you know about him as a person?" asked Lucy.

"Not much really. We didn't tend to socialise outside of work. He never went to social events – not even the Christmas lunch."

"Did you find that a bit odd?"

"Not really. He was a very private, shy person. Kept himself to himself as it were."

"So he wasn't close to anyone?"

"Not to my knowledge."

Lucy was silent, listening to this exchange and thinking.

"What about his girlfriend?" asked Lucy after some time.

"Girlfriend? He didn't have one."

"Oh but we thought…." Lucy began until Mick dug her in the ribs, warning her to be quiet.

"I'm surprised you should query that as I was convinced he was gay. He was very effeminate in his actions."

"Was he interested in anyone?"

"There was someone but I'm not sure Ashley was interested though. This one guy who wasn't in the closet always seemed to be following Ashley with his eyes."

"Have you got a name?"

"I'm not sure if I should." Seeing the look that passed between Mick and Lucy she added, "I don't want to cause any trouble, it might have been perfectly innocent."

"We won't pass it on," assured Mick.

"Well, ok. Bernard. He's a bit of an odd fish actually."

"On the subject of this fraud, what was that about?"

"Ashley had stumbled across three or four colleagues who seemed to be mixing up finances. Money disappeared regularly and they kept claiming expenses which couldn't be real. He came to me eventually after he'd been watching for sometime."

"What did you do about it?"

"Nothing. We wanted more evidence before whistleblowing."

"Was this Bernard involved?"

"I don't know. Ashley didn't mention his name." Helen looked down as she said this.

Lucy, a bit suspicious, tried to catch Mick's eye but he seemed to be deliberately avoiding her. This had been the only time Helen had seemed cagey and stopped making eye contact. If Mick had noticed it he wasn't letting it be known.

"Do you know Belinda?"

"No. Should I?"

"Not necessarily. I'm picking up from this that you didn't really know Ashley that well. You haven't told us yet why he lost his job."

"He decided to tell the managers about the fraud he was convinced was happening. I had warned him to wait but he wouldn't. I felt we needed more evidence as we didn't really have anything."

"Why would this cause him to lose his job?"

"Those concerned had covered their tracks very well. Too well actually as they had made it look as if Ashley was the one committing fraud."

"How did they know he had given the game away?"

Helen shrugged, unable to answer, but said, "I assume he must have said something to someone and it had got back to the real culprits."

"That would have been a bit stupid of him and from what you say he was far from that."

"I'm not so sure. He did speak about letting them have the opportunity to stop so he wouldn't have to say anything. I advised caution of course but he must have gone ahead with it."

There was silence between the three of them. No one knew how to respond to what Helen had revealed.

Helen looked at her watch and jumped to her feet. "Sorry I'm going to be late back if I don't hurry. Please remember, this didn't come from me if this gets out."

"Thank you we appreciate the time you've taken to speak to us," said Mick rising to his feet as well.

"Well what did you think," asked Mick when Helen had gone.

"I'm not sure. At one point I thought she was telling us a load of lies. Telling us what she wanted us to believe."

"I did wonder but decided not to challenge her. We don't know if we can trust her or how much she may have been involved. She obviously made herself look good if she is in fact a murderer."

"Hmm," said Lucy. "Where does this leave us and our investigation?"

"Not sure at the moment. I think we need to be clear and weigh up what she told us with what we already know. This might help show us where to go next."

"Maybe Ellie will be able to help. She'll only have what we tell us no body language or tone of voice from Helen to influence her thoughts."

"You're right as usual. That sounds a good idea. Ellie should come round to ours tonight then."

"She usually does anyway."

"Very true. I don't know why she bothered finding herself a flat as she spends so much time at ours."

"She wanted that independence."

"So why spend so much time with us?"

"I don't know. I hadn't even thought about it. She knew she was welcome to stay."

"Mind you if she had I would have gone insane with the two of you getting at each other all the time."

"Get on with you. You know you love it really."

"Very true," said Mick grinning. He was very fond of Ellie and loved the close bond she shared with Lucy and therefore with him as well.

He was grateful that Lucy had her to turn to should something happen to him. The recent heart attack had brought home to him that he wouldn't live forever. His Lucy wouldn't be on her own should the worst happen. He wasn't telling Lucy but the doctors had warned him that his heart was weakened and he could have another attack at any time. His heart was wearing out and he was becoming like an elderly man at only fifty five. He knew there was a big possibility that he wouldn't be going back to work. Knowing Lucy really needed to be told the truth of the situation was too much for Mick, who was a coward and hated to upset Lucy as such news surely would.

Chapter Eighteen

"How did it go with Helen?" queried Ellie on the way home with Lucy.

"Wait until we get home then you can hear the news from both of us."

"You mean you got somewhere?"

"Sort of."

Opening the front door Lucy called to Mick to let him know they were home. Getting no response she went directly to the living room without taking her coat and shoes off or putting her bag down, the usual routine when getting home.

She rushed to Mick in alarm when she saw him ghostly white. Ellie, close on her heels also hurried to Mick's side. His eyes were closed, alarming the pair. Ellie, slightly removed from the situation immediately felt for his pulse. Good, he was at least alive.

"Mick, Mick, can you hear me?" asked Ellie.

No response.

"I think you should call an ambulance," said Ellie to her friend who was stood motionless, terror written all over her face.

"Lucy come on, get a grip, Mick needs you right now," said Ellie sharply to her friend.

Lucy still didn't respond so Ellie decided she was the one to be proactive. She reached for her phone in her bag and pulled it out, starting to press buttons for the emergency services. She paused as she heard a faint voice saying, "I'm ok, just tired out."

"You don't look it," said Ellie.

"It's ok."

"I'm still calling the paramedics out. It won't do any harm to check you over."

Mick, feeling too weak didn't argue. Part of him was afraid this was it. He'd had chest pains on and off since arriving back home.

The doorbell rang just minutes later and Ellie went to admit the paramedics. Quickly assessing the situation they got to work. "You need to come with us," said one of them.

Mick shook his head. If he were to die he wanted it to be quietly at home with the women he loved not at hospital, surrounded by staff and hooked up to beeping machines.

"Please," said Ellie. "For Lucy's sake you need to go. She needs you around for sometime yet. I need you as well. We need to solve this mystery."

"Is that the one you were telling us about?" asked the paramedic.

Ellie nodded.

"It maybe you've just overdone it after being out of hospital so recently. We do need to make sure though."

Mick was too worn out to argue further and allowed himself to be led out to the ambulance and strapped on to the trolley. Lucy got in behind him and Ellie made her way to her car to meet them in A and E.

Mick was hastily taken to the resus unit to be closely monitored. It was a relief to Lucy and Ellie to realise it was not another heart attack but was close. Mick was to be admitted overnight for observation and possibly going home the next day. The two women were given a good talking to by the doctor who was not impressed that Mick had gone out that day when he was supposed to be resting and taking it easy at home for some time to come.

"He insisted," said Lucy. "Also I didn't know he was strictly confined to the house for the present. He really had seemed so much better."

"He has been warned that he was to take it very easy as another heart attack wasn't out of the question."

Lucy paled, not having realised this.

"I see you didn't know," commented the doctor.

Lucy and Ellie both shook their heads.

"If we had known believe me he wouldn't have gone anywhere," said Lucy. "I would have made sure of that." Lucy was very firm in her words. "When he's back home I won't let him lift a finger that's for sure.

The doctor knew Lucy was speaking truth and was happy with the situation. He confirmed again that providing there was no change then Mick would be discharged tomorrow. He was now certain that Mick would no longer have the opportunity to overdo things if he was any judge of character and he wasn't often wrong about someone.

"Why didn't you tell me what the doctors had told you? How could you risk your health – no, your life like that?" Lucy barraged Mick with questions until Ellie hushed her up.

"Can't you see he's tired and in pain. The questions can wait until he's feeling better."

"I'm sorry," whispered Mick. "I didn't want you to worry. I couldn't bear to see that look on your face every time you looked at me."

Lucy nodded, not trusting herself to speak. She wanted desperately to throw her arms around her husband but the leads attached to him wouldn't let her.

"I'll be ok. I really did feel well enough to go and meet Helen with you. In future I'll stick to phone calls and advising you two."

"You really think you'll get that chance? You are resting and nothing else."

"I can still use my brain and talk."

"Come on Lucy we should leave Mick to rest now," said Ellie.

"I can't leave him what happens if he deteriorates and I'm not here?"

"They'd ring you and I would bring you straight here. The best thing you can do is let Mick sleep."

Lucy allowed herself to be led away, very reluctantly.

"We'll stop off at yours to pick up your night things then we're going back to mine."

"But you're further away from the hospital if there's a problem."

"It didn't matter last time. This time he isn't in immediate danger."

Lucy saw the sense in this and agreed with the plan. She wasn't thinking clearly having had such a nasty shock. She really had no idea how weakened her husband had become. Now she had questions going round in her mind. Would he work again? Was he ever going to be back to his old self? Would she have to give up work to look after him?

Ellie, seeing her friend was lost in thought left her in silence. She knew Lucy would have a lot to work through and it would take time to get her head around things. Ellie saw more clearly than Lucy, possibly because she was removed slightly from the situation. She wasn't sure Mick would ever get back to work. The doctor had been implying such a scenario. He was going to have to take care for the foreseeable future, maybe for the rest of his life. Mick had been so ill it had left him permanently weakened.

Ellie felt sorry for Lucy and frustrated as well. This could all have been avoided if the situation had been properly spelled out to them. It wasn't just Mick's fault for not following instructions but the staff as well for not ensuring Lucy was fully informed of the realities now facing them.

Once at home Lucy went straight to bed without a word to Ellie. She wasn't meaning to be rude or shut her friend out, she was just trying to process the information she had received and what it meant for herself and the future. She had pretty much decided she would hand in her notice at work so she could concentrate on Mick. She didn't know how they would manage without any income but was sure something could be worked out.

Ellie, like Lucy, spent a sleepless night tossing and turning, everything they had heard going round and round in their minds. Ellie could hear the creaks of the springs in Lucy's bed as she moved around, so Ellie knew her friend was awake as well. Hoping Lucy might eventually fall asleep Ellie left her alone.

Morning eventually came, after a night that seemed to go on forever. Both got up with bruises under their eyes and a pallor to their faces. Ellie phoned in sick for both of them. She was determined not to leave Lucy or Mick alone, she needed to be there for both of them. They had done so much for her and now it was her turn to return the favour, plus they were such close friends she couldn't leave them to face this alone.

As soon as they were up and dressed they made their way to the hospital even though it wasn't visiting time. Lucy was just hoping they would be allowed in especially if Mick was to be discharged. She sat in the car staring straight ahead in silence. She noticed nothing they drove passed. Ellie, seeing this, was glad she was driving. She was tired but was more able to concentrate and focus than Lucy obviously was.

"Sorry you can't come in," said the nurse as the women tried to get into the ward.

"We came to see Mick," explained Ellie. "This is his wife Lucy. We were told he would be discharged today if he were stable."

"The doctor won't be doing his rounds until after his outpatient clinic so it won't be until this afternoon at the earliest. You should go away and come back in later during visiting time. We should know more then."

Seeing nothing for it, Ellie took hold of Lucy's arm and led her away. Lucy remained unfocused, staring straight ahead.

"Come on, we'll see if we can get something to eat and drink in the cafe if it's open," said Ellie.

Lucy didn't reply and gave no sign that she'd even heard correctly.

They made their way there with Ellie leading the way, still holding on to Lucy as they went.

The café was indeed open and Ellie sat Lucy down at a table and went to place their order.

"Two coffees please and can we have two croissants as well."

"Your friend looks as if she's not well," commented the assistant behind the counter.

"She's had a shock," said Ellie, not willing to divulge more at that time. Besides, it wasn't any of her business.

"Sugar is good for that, put plenty of sugar in the coffee. Soon sort her out that will."

Ellie nodded but said nothing.

Taking the tray to the table she took a seat next to her friend. Finding the cup and plate placed in front of her Lucy automatically began eating and drinking. She didn't taste anything and showed no enjoyment but Ellie was pleased to see some colour coming back to her friend's face. A sense of relief washed over her. She was sure now that Lucy would be all right. All she had to do now was get Lucy talking and worry about Mick.

"Thank you," said Lucy quietly. "It was just what I needed."

"Do you want another coffee?" asked Ellie.

"No thanks," said Lucy shaking her head.

"What shall we do for the rest of the morning until visiting time this afternoon?"

Lucy shrugged.

"We could wander around the shops. It's ages since we've done that. We always have a laugh."

Lucy shook her head saying, "I'm not in the mood."

"Well what do you fancy doing."

"I don't know, that's the problem."

"We can't sit here all day and I don't want you to mope around doing nothing. It won't help you and it will just make the time go slower."

"Why don't we go back to yours and look at the information we have so far. We might be able to take this further you never know."

Ellie was taken by surprise. This was the last thing she had expected to hear but thinking about it was probably the ideal thing to take their minds off their circumstances and concentrate on the case at hand. If they were lucky they might be able to move things further forward, although she was in no doubt they were far from solving it. She sensed they hadn't even met the perpetrator as yet. She didn't know why she thought this, it had just popped into her mind out of nowhere.

They arrived home to find Tammy looking out the window. When they got out of the car Tammy opened her window and called to them.

"Is everything all right," called Tammy. "You're not usually here at this time of day?"

"It's Mick, he had a funny turn last night and is back in hospital. He should be home later today when the doctor has been round. We can go back during visiting time and see what the verdict is."

"I'm so sorry," she replied looking at Lucy.

Lucy acknowledged her with a brief nod but made no response.

"Thank you," said Ellie, walking passed, holding on to Lucy as she did so guiding her forward.

Settled once more on the comfy sofa they looked at the information they had in front of them. There wasn't really much to go on except for what they had learned from Helen.

"We need to speak to Bernard," said Ellie and Lucy nodded in agreement.

Although still very quiet Lucy was much more with it now. This had been a good idea to look at the case even though they were both obviously very tired from a sleepless night.

"I wonder if Tammy has heard Ashley mention the name?" said Ellie.

"We could ask her," said Lucy.

"Not now. Let's go through what we know first, It might just give us more information and form more questions for Tammy."

"We still don't know if Helen is legitimate or not. She could be leading us on a wild goose chase."

"We have to assume she's on the level for now. What else can we do when we know nothing of Ashley and his life. If we are to investigate we have to trust what we are told unless it's proven otherwise."

"Another thought, how are we to contact this Bernard. We don't know anything about him and remember it could be him or he could be heartbroken at the loss of Ashley."

"This is so complicated."

"It would be. It's because we don't know anyone involved or where to start."

Lucy glanced at her watch and cried, "Gosh look at the time. If we don't get going we'll miss the start of visiting time."

Ellie stood up pleased with herself. She had been aware of the time but hadn't wanted to say anything. Lucy had definitely been distracted which had been the whole point of the exercise.

The two women got themselves together and went to Ellie's car.

"Don't get your hopes up too much as they may decide to keep him in longer or the consultant might not have been on his rounds yet," said Ellie as she drove to the hospital.

"But they said he could leave."

"But that wasn't the consultant. He may have other ideas."

"I hadn't thought of that."

"I just wanted you to be aware. The reality is Mick must still be quite unwell." Ellie hated seeing Lucy's face cloud over in the way it did at that last remark, but it needed saying.

Lucy said nothing, trying to fight the tears that welled up in her eyes. Ellie saw it and reached out to touch her friends arm.

"Why does life have to be so difficult?" questioned Lucy as they reached the hospital.

"I wish I had the answer to that. I'd be a millionaire by now and would have stopped work."

Lucy smiled, unable to help herself despite her worry over Mick. Ellie saw it and was satisfied. Lucy wasn't so lost that she'd lost her sense of humour.

On the ward Lucy rushed ahead of Ellie eager to see her husband. He was sat in the chair next to the bed, dressed and not attached to any machines. He smiled and stood up when he saw the two women approach.

"I'm coming home," he announced. "The consultant wants to speak to us together though."

Lucy's face clouded over.

"It's not bad news," said Mick. "He just wants to make sure we understand the situation to avoid a reoccurrence."

The three walked down the ward to where a nurse was standing on the phone. "I've just let the consultant know you're here. He's on his way."

They sat down and waited for him to arrive. Five minutes then ten minutes passed and no doctor. Even Ellie was starting to get anxious and it showed in her face. She leaned across Mick to speak to Lucy who was sat on his other side, when the consultant walked through the door.

"I'm so sorry to keep you. I got held up with a query about another patient. Ok if you follow me we'll talk in private."

He led them to the day room which was empty at that time. Ellie wondered what private meant if they were to talk in a public place where patients and visitors could be wandering in and out.

The four of them sat down. The consultant looked at Ellie and asked Mick and Lucy, "Are you happy for this lady to hear what we say?"

Lucy responded, "She's a very close friend. I want her to hear this."

Mick also nodded his approval.

"Now we've agreed that I want you to know that although Mick is stable now he was very ill and we didn't expect him to pull through. He has but he needs to take it very easy as he could have another attack at any time. His heart is quite a bit weakened and physically he isn't strong. He needs almost complete rest to improve the condition of his heart and to get his strength back. I must warn you that he may not get back to his former fitness levels. For now he needs to stay at home but can potter about a bit. We'll see what he's like at his next appointment in four weeks time."

"Is he….is he…." Lucy couldn't get the words out and at the same time wasn't sure she wanted to hear the answer.

"He's not in any danger at the moment and shouldn't be as long as he follows orders this time." The doctor stopped and looked severely at Mick who blushed.

"But I can do sedentary things that use my brain can't I?" asked Mick, wanting to make sure for the women's sake that he could be involved in the case as an armchair detective.

"Yes, there is no reason why not. Your brain is fine, it's your heart I'm more concerned about at the moment."

"Thank you," said Ellie, seeing that Lucy was lost for words. She was struggling to take in all that she had heard.

The consultant nodded and stood up, his job done. He was sure now that Mick would indeed be taking it easy having seen the look on Lucy's face. It wasn't the first time a patient hadn't followed instructions because their partner wasn't told the reality of the situation. He understood completely that enforced rest was a completely new lifestyle that was alien to the nature of most people.

Ellie looked at her watch and suggested, "Shall we get a cup of coffee in the cafeteria?"

"I'd rather get Mick straight home to be honest," said Lucy.

"That's fine," said Ellie having thought that would be the case.

They walked out to the car Mick leaning heavily on Lucy for support.

"Do you want me to bring the car over?"

"It's fine," said Mick not wanting to be a nuisance in spite of the difficulty he was having. He already felt breathless. He didn't want to be ill again but didn't want anyone to know just how ill he was feeling.

"I think I'll bring the car over," said Ellie seeing the struggle Mick was having. Privately she wasn't sure he should have been allowed home but she wasn't going to voice that thought.

Mick, relieved he wouldn't have to walk any further stopped and watched Ellie hurry to get the car. He just hoped he wouldn't collapse before getting home and on to the sofa. He hadn't admitted to staff how ill he was feeling, worried he wouldn't be allowed home. Unknown to the three friends the consultant was watching out of the window and saw the struggle Mick seemed to be having. He hoped he'd done the right thing by discharging Mick so soon.

Mick doubled over trying to take deep breaths but failing. He felt he was on the verge of fainting due to the breathlessness. It was at this point that Ellie drew up to the pavement and got out. She was concerned to see the grey look that Mick had taken up.

"Are you sure you're ok?" asked Ellie with some concern.

"I'll be fine once we're in the car and I'm home," said Mick with a confidence he didn't feel.

The two women manoeuvred Mick into the car and Ellie took to the wheel and drove off. She kept glancing at Mick and was pleased to see the colour get back into his face.

It wasn't long before they drew up outsight Mick and Lucy's house. Ellie got out as well and went around the front to help Lucy get Mick inside.

"Are you sure you don't want us to help you to bed?" queried Lucy, speaking for the first time in a while.

Placing Mick on the sofa Ellie turned to go saying, "I'm off. Let me know in a few days if you want a lift to work."

"I don't intend going for the foreseeable future. I'm going to stay here for now and watch Mick."

Unsurprised Ellie nodded and left the house. She got back home and collapsed on the sofa. She felt exhausted so she hated to think how Mick must be feeling. The whole situation was one hundred percent draining.

Chapter Nineteen

The days passed in a blur to Lucy who spent all day looking after Mick and half the night awake with worry. She didn't want Mick to know this as he was sleeping well but Mick couldn't help but notice the swelling and bruising under her eyes which told their own story.

"You should go back to work," he suggested one day a few weeks later.

Lucy shook her head and yawned.

"You need to get out, get some fresh air at least. It's not doing you any good staying in with me. I'll be fine if you leave me food and drink available."

Lucy again shook her head. She was so terrified of losing Mick that she didn't want to leave him even for a second. She knew she was being irrational but she had received a nasty shock when the consultant had spoken to them.

"You're looking tired love. You need a break. Ring Ellie see if you can go round for an hour or so."

"She'll be at work, it's the middle of the day."

"It's Saturday."

Lucy shook her head. How could she have made that mistake. She really wasn't with it.

"Go on give her a ring. It's obvious you could do with it."

Lucy nodded reluctantly and picked up her phone.

Ellie was enthusiastic with her response as she too, had been worrying about her friend who had no time or inclination to do anything. She sensed that Mick may have finally put his foot down and insisted. She'd missed her friend having not seen her since Mick came home. Lucy had even been reluctant to let Ellie visit in case it was too much for Mick. They'd had no chance to even discuss the case so hadn't got much further with it.

Ellie had spent some time with Tammy but had stayed off the subject of Ashley, deciding to wait until she could discuss the situation further. She hoped that seeing Lucy today might take things forward a bit, or maybe Lucy would just want to relax and take it easy and if so that would be fine as well.

There had been no further reports in the media as to whether the police were still working on the case so she assumed no arrest had taken place. Not that it didn't mean anything as they could have suspicions but no evidence to actually prove it.

It wasn't long before the doorbell rang. Ellie let Lucy in trying not to show how shocked she was at her friends appearance. It was clear that Lucy hadn't bothered too much even about coming out to visit her. She was quite unkempt in appearance and the pale face with bruises under her eyes told Ellie so much. She felt sorry for her friend and wished she'd take it easy on herself. She knew her friend was punishing herself for Mick being taken ill a second time.

"Do you want to go into town? We could have a wander and then have lunch somewhere."

Lucy shook her head as expected and said, "I can't be away from Mick that long. I thought I'd only pop around for an hour."

Ellie was disappointed but not surprised. She was going to have her work cut out that was for sure. She was determined that her friend had to get out more. She understood Lucy not wanting to go back to work but doing nothing at all….

"How is Mick doing?"

"He's ok, but I'm not letting him lift a finger. He sits on the sofa all day and I wait on him."

"I'm sure he could get up and make himself a cup of tea, that's not going to strain him too much."

Lucy was adamant that he wasn't to do anything.

"I think you're taking things to extremes Lucy."

"Maybe it was a mistake me coming here. I should get back." Lucy stood up.

"I'm sorry if I'm upsetting you but it has to be said. He doesn't have to be a complete invalid. That isn't what the consultant meant."

"He might have a heart attack while I'm out and I'd never forgive myself," said Lucy close to tears that she wasn't being understood.

Ellie couldn't respond to that and reluctantly let Lucy out. Knowing Mick was free for at least ten minutes she sent him a text.

Her phone rang a minute later.

"I'm sorry you couldn't persuade her," said Mick when she answered.

"So am I. How are you anyway?"

"I'm fine. I just wish she'd stop fussing around me all the time. It's as if I have to walk on egg shells. She is just taking the situation to extremes. I suggested she leaves food and drink for me while she goes out, but that's unacceptable as well." Mick sighed.

"I don't know what to suggest," said Ellie feeling at a loss.

"Neither do I. I'll just have to keep working on her. I'm worried she'll collapse herself soon. It would help if she were to sleep at nights but she isn't. She thinks I'm asleep but I'm only pretending. She's so restless, tossing and turning, she wakes me up."

"That's not good," said Ellie concerned.

"Look I've got to go. She's back," said Mick abruptly before disconnecting the call.

"You're back early," he commented when Lucy walked in.

"I couldn't stop thinking about you. I just couldn't leave you. It didn't feel right."

Mick had nothing to say to that. Instead he changed the subject. "I thought maybe you'd discuss the case further with Ellie."

"I can't when you are on my mind all the time. It didn't seem right."

"Maybe Ellie should come around here and we could go over it together. Time is passing by which could make it harder to solve the case. The murderer could have covered their tracks by now and have a solid alibi."

"It might be too much for you. I don't want you to tire yourself out."

"I'm capable of more than you give me credit for love," he said gently. "When I get tired I can say so. Or I could go to bed while you two talk down here. There are ways around the situation."

Lucy shook her head. "I don't think so. It's not worth the risk."

"Well ok, if you're not comfortable with that why not invite Ellie for a meal. You are neglecting her these days."

"She understands. She knows you have to be my priority at the moment."

"She doesn't have a choice does she with you taking that attitude."

"Please don't fight me on this. You gave me such a fright I can't lose you."

"I understand that. I really do but I'm ok. You don't have to be around at all times anymore. I'm getting stronger I can feel it. I'm sure the doctor will let me get out a bit next week at my appointment."

"No, no way. I'm not letting you out."

"I can't stay in indefinitely. It's like I'm a prisoner in my own home."

"It's for your own good."

"Not if the doctor says I can get out a bit and start doing stuff around the house."

Lucy shook her head but didn't respond. She didn't want to be the cause of another heart attack.

Mick realising he was getting nowhere decided he'd have to bring it up at his appointment as he was sure she no longer needed to be around at all times. He was stronger than he'd been when he went out before so was sure it would be ok if he took things gently.

Chapter Twenty

"What's happening about finding who killed Ashley?" asked Tammy when she next saw Ellie.

"Nothing at the moment, not since that scare with Mick."

"But that was weeks ago."

"I know, but Lucy won't hear of any talk about it. She won't leave Mick alone for even a second. I'm sure she panics when she just goes to the loo."

"That sounds a bit extreme."

"I know."

"Well look, if she won't, why don't we get on with it. At least I know a bit about Ashley and the people involved. I might be able to be of use."

"But you're not well yourself. I don't want you getting too exhausted."

"I'll be fine if I pace myself. We can do it in short bursts. Anyway I'm having a good patch at the moment."

"I had realised, I think. You have been much more able to talk and I've seen more of you."

"Yes, I can't get out but I can make phone calls and we can discuss things."

"You know I think you have a good idea. Why don't we give it a go."

Tammy smiled at her new friend. The two had become closer over the time that Lucy had been in her self imposed exile. Tammy was pleased as she had been so lonely. Her old friends had given up on her long ago that to have someone was good for her. It took her mind off herself for awhile. She wasn't stupid, she knew Ellie would always be closest to Lucy but to know they could be friends was good for her.

Ellie felt the same. She no longer believed Tammy could be the guilty party. She also no longer thought of her as weird having a skeleton in the flat. Maybe Tammy was just a bit eccentric but that was fine. Everyone was different.

"The last thing we looked into was where Ashley had last worked. We wanted to know why he had lost his job."

"Did you find anything out?" asked Tammy eagerly.

"Well yes, in a way. Mick and Lucy spoke to an HR personnel who met with them and mentioned fraud taking place. We were unsure if Ashley was mixed up in it or if he knew who it was and was going to blow the whistle."

"That would give a motive for murder straight away."

"Exactly."

"A man called Bernard was mentioned. Have you heard the name at all."

Tammy looked blank as she thought about it, before shaking her head. It meant nothing to her. "Do you think Bernard is the killer or the lover."

"I don't have a clue. I really no nothing. Lucy and Mick didn't say anything much so I don't think they were any further forward except with the name. I remember us saying we needed to find out more about him and hopefully get to speak to him."

"As I'm not known to the company or to this Helen why don't I ring tomorrow and find out if I can speak to him."

"Great idea. We need to move this case forward if we are to solve it ourselves."

"It will be a miracle when neither of us know much."

"You still know more than me as you at least knew Ashley."

"But that's all and knowing Belinda a bit helps but not a great deal."

"Well, we can only work with what we've got so let's take it from here and see what happens."

"Agreed," said Tammy happily. She was so pleased to have something to do to occupy her time. Even if she couldn't do much, she could think about what they knew which was just as important aa the leg work. She felt a bit guilty that a lot of it would fall to Ellie but there was nothing she could do about that. Ellie knew what the situation was and was still happy to work together so it was obvious Ellie didn't mind.

………

"Oh hello yes, I was hoping to speak to Bernard. Is he around at all?" asked Tammy, trying to speak in a posh sort of voice to disguise who she was a bit.

"Who's speaking?"

"Amanda."

"Ok Amanda just transferring you now."

"Hello can I help?" asked a female voice.

"Uh I was expecting to speak to Bernard."

"Who is this?" The voice on the other end was sounding suspicious which got Tammy a bit worried. She was glad she'd given a false name. It might turn out to be safer.

"Amanda. I'm his girlfriend."

"Oh well, I'm afraid he's not here."

"Oh I was sure he was working today at least that's what he said last night," said Tammy thinking quickly. She hadn't expected this. She paused before asking, "Can I leave a message?"

"I don't think that's a good idea."

"Oh? Why not?"

"It just isn't. Now if there's nothing more I can help you with." With that the phone went dead and Tammy was left staring at the phone.

Well, that hadn't been very helpful. She had achieved a big fat zero. Was Bernard there or not? Who had she been speaking to? She wished she'd had the sense to ask at least she might have a name to go on to tell Ellie later when she dropped in. Wishing she could start the call again she lay there thinking. If only she could come up with another reason to ring but she couldn't risk it in case she spoke to the same people and they recognised her voice. Maybe Ellie could ring but that could also be unhelpful and raise suspicions if Bernard didn't often receive calls.

Something about the situation worried Tammy. She was concerned that Bernard might have lost his job. If so, then the chances were likely that he had met the same fate as Ashley. She didn't know if her imagination was running away with her again but she couldn't get the thought out of her mind. The fact that she couldn't speak to Bernard or leave a message for him was suspicious. It could also indicate that the female she was speaking to could be the killer. At least they knew nothing about her. She had covered herself sufficiently enough for them to be unable to identify her.

....

Ellie could see at a glance that Tammy had achieved nothing by the look on her face.

"What happened?"

"Not a lot, except being put through to a female who didn't identify herself who said Bernard wasn't there and wouldn't let me leave a message for him. I said I was his girlfriend and gave the name Amanda."

"That was clever of you," said Ellie. "I would never have thought of that in a million years."

Tammy blushed. "Not really. I didn't intend doing that it just came out."

"Well done. Under the circumstances it was for the best, even though we are no further forward."

"Well we could be if we could find out where Bernard lived at least we would know if he had met the same fate as Ashley. There have been no reports of anymore dead males turning up so I'm not convinced."

"True, but they might have just hidden the body better this time."

"You seem certain he's dead."

Tammy looked serious and nodded. "I have this horrible feeling inside. It started when I found out he wasn't there."

"It might not mean anything. He might just be on holiday."

"Why didn't they just tell me that?"

"Because you played the part of his girlfriend and you would have known if he were away. They would have been suspicious of you. Besides, if he really was gay and fancied Ashley then it was unlikely he would have a girlfriend anyway."

Tammy's face fell, she hadn't thought of that. How could she have been so stupid?

"Don't beat yourself up," said Ellie interpreting Tammy's face correctly. "You were clever to think up a false story on the spur of the moment like that."

"Maybe, but I still messed up."

"I don't think so. We are slightly further forward. What I'm going to do is see if Lucy will ring and speak to Helen again and find out more about Bernard, maybe even get an address for him."

"Do you think Lucy will?"

"I don't see why not. It makes sense for her to do it as she has met Helen. I think it was possible you spoke to Helen today. It's a pity you didn't get a name."

"I didn't think to ask for the name to be honest."

"No problem. Let me speak to Lucy."

Ellie got out her phone and quickly got the call going through to Lucy. Ellie let it ring with no response. A look of concern came over her face. Lucy should have been able to speak as she was at home as far as Ellie knew. Ellie left a message. She hoped Lucy wasn't deliberately ignoring her after the way they had left things when Lucy had left so abruptly. She also hoped Mick was ok. That could be another reason for Lucy to stay silent.

Tammy said, "You look worried."

"I am. It's not like Lucy to ignore a call."

"Could Mick have a hospital appointment."

"That's a point. I'd forgotten. I knew Mick had said something about an appointment coming up. That must be it." Relief spread across her face.

Tammy felt good to have thought of it. She didn't like to think of her new friend worrying like that. She realised there could be legitimate reason for the concern though. Although she didn't say anything she still couldn't see why Lucy couldn't answer the phone. Mobiles were precisely that, used anywhere.

"Is there anything else we could do until we get word from Lucy?" asked Tammy. She was itching to get on with it. In her mind it had been left too long already.

"I'm not sure unless we chase Belinda up and find out about her lies."

"I could do that now," said Tammy.

"Query with her why she said Ashley went to his parents."

Tammy nodded and reached for her phone. "Oh hello Belinda, it's Tammy. I was wondering how Ashley's parents are coping with the news."

"What news? Who is this?"

"Tammy, Ashley's friend and neighbour."

"Oh Tammy, sorry I can't talk." The phone went dead.

"I take it that didn't go well," said Ellie as Tammy put the phone down.

Tammy shook her head. She was very abrupt and said she couldn't talk when I said who I was. I suppose I shouldn't have been surprised. She didn't want me involved with you or the case, she made that very clear."

"I remember now. Sorry, if I had used my brain I wouldn't have suggested you phone her. Although it does mean we will never get answers to our questions."

"Does it matter. Surely knowing about Bernard means we are further forward and no longer need Belinda anyway."

"I'm not sure. I think it could be important to know why she pretended Ashley was with his parents when they are no longer alive. She must be involved somewhere or why lie. Surely she would be worried about his disappearance as well. I know they had broken up but even so....."

"I understand what you say but she can't be involved because of Bernard."

"Why not?" asked Ellie.

"Well because….actually I don't know."

"Well then. We need to hear from Lucy…." Ellie stopped speaking as her phone rang. A glance told her it was her friend.

"Hi Lucy, I was worried when you didn't take the call."

"We were at the hospital with the consultant."

"How did it go?"

"Well according to him it's ok for Mick to do a bit around the house again. He is doing well and should be capable of doing light work such as making a cup of tea."

"That's great. Does that mean you can come back to work," asked Ellie, unable to keep the delight out of her voice.

"I suppose so but I'm still not sure about leaving him. What if something were to happen."

"Ok if that seems like too much you could come to me for an hour or so in the evening so you are out and can see how well Mick can cope."

"I suppose so. They are talking about Mick getting out and about a bit after his next appointment."

"That sounds really good," said an enthusiastic Ellie.

"I'm not sure I could ever agree with that, not after last time."

"I understand that and I know you had a nasty shock but this time he must be genuinely improving or the doctor wouldn't sanction it."

"I suppose you're right. Anyway I have to go now as I want to get Mick home."

"Sorry I wouldn't have kept you talking. Ring me when you get home and I'll update you on the case."

"What case?" asked Lucy genuinely puzzled.

"You know, Ashley?"

"Oh yeah that. I really think it's best to forget it and leave it to the police. My thoughts are with Mick at the moment."

"I don't think Mick would agree with you. He would be eager for us to continue."

"It's not up to him, it's me. I'm the one who has to pick up the pieces when he overdoes it."

"All I want is for you to ring and speak to Helen and enquire about Bernard. Tammy has spoken to someone who says he isn't there so we are worried he may have met the same end as Ashley."

"We…ll I suppose I could do that. It can't do any harm. I'll do it when we get home and get back to you with her response."

Ellie looked at Tammy after putting the phone down. "She's going to do it but it looked as if she wouldn't at first. She doesn't want to continue with the case so it might have to be the two of us."

"That's not a good idea as it puts most of it on you alone because I can't get out. I wouldn't be able to go to check out Bernard and I wouldn't want you to go on your own."

"I see your point. We can try and see where it gets us. Maybe given a few days Lucy will start to realise that Mick is doing well and can be left alone now."

"That's great news."

"I know but Lucy still thinks she needs to be with him permanently."

"We have to remember she had a nasty shock. She needs to accept that Mick is now on the road to recovery as long as he follows orders and takes it slowly."

"You're right I know."

"I'm always right," said Tammy.

"Oh yeah, since when?"

"Uh, I'm not sure maybe never."

The two women laughed. Ellie was amazed at how close she now felt to Tammy. She could have similar conversations as with Lucy and Tammy would join in laughing. She was glad she'd met Tammy and had a chance to get to know her properly. She had been lonely at first with Lucy being so tied up with Mick.

Ellie's phone started to ring. Picking it up she said, "Hi Lucy. How did you get on?"

"Well, she was surprisingly forthcoming. I hadn't expected to get anywhere with her to be honest. Bernard lives at 2 Brickhill Close."

"Where's that? I don't recognise the address at all."

"It's near me off of Westview Lane."

"Great I'll go around there tomorrow afternoon after lunch. Do you want to come with me. If it's so close you won't be leaving Mick for very long."

"I'm not sure. I'll let you know."

"Ok I'll ring you just before I leave and see if you want to come."

"Good luck with it," said Lucy and rang off without any further words.

Ellie looked at the phone. "Well, that was a bit abrupt. She didn't say bye or even answer me."

"She seems to have changed from what you're saying and what I remember of her."

Ellie nodded, looking sad. She was trying to hold back the tears and couldn't trust herself to speak. She wasn't sufficiently close to Tammy to reveal her true feelings.

Tammy noticed and said nothing. She reached out a hand and took Ellie's in hers.

"She'll come around you'll see. She won't throw years of friendship down the drain. It would mean too much for her to do that."

"I hope you're right. I think she blames me for the scare with Mick last time as she has hardly spoken since then and has been a bit off with me when we do speak."

"I'm sure it's nothing but worry over Mick."

"Maybe. Anyway, I really should go and let you rest. I'll pop in after trying Bernard tomorrow and let you know how it goes."

"I wish I could come with you."

"I know, but you are better staying here. You can be the brains behind the operation."

"Brains? That sounds good. I'm official."

"Of course you are."

Tammy was left with a smile on her face when Ellie had left. It was good to feel part of something even if she couldn't join in fully. She felt sorry for Lucy but was glad things had turned out like this as she would have still been lonely and feeling on the outside of life. She felt guilty but couldn't help how she felt. She had been jealous of Ellie and Lucy's close friendship but now had hopes that they would fully include her when Lucy was back in life again.

Chapter Twenty One

Ellie stopped outside Lucy's house and honked the horn. She was so pleased that Lucy had agreed to go with her, talked into it by Mick who was desperate to have some alone time.

"It's so good to see you," said Ellie beaming, when Lucy got in the passenger seat.

"Yes," said Lucy.

Oh dear, thought Ellie, this wasn't going to plan. She had imagined them talking rapidly having so much to say but it wasn't to be.

"Right let's go."

Silence from Lucy who didn't even ask if she needed to direct Ellie. In fact the silence was stony. There was no comfortable feeling for the two friends. Ellie began to wish she hadn't asked Lucy to come along if she was going to be like this. Things had last been this bad when Ellie had begun to suspect Lucy of murdering Phyliss. Even then it hadn't gone on this long. She didn't know what to say so the silence continued.

Lucy had no wish to start talking. She had been badly hurt by Ellie who didn't seem to understand how she needed to be with Mick at all times. Lucy was only there because Mick had insisted, otherwise she wouldn't have come. She wanted nothing more to do with Ellie and this time there was no way they would make up and get back to the way they were.

Mick couldn't understand the two women and wanted to knock their heads together. If only they could start talking again. This had been the main reason he had insisted Lucy should go with Ellie to check on Bernard. He had thought if they were shut in the car together they would have to talk. He hadn't reckoned with Lucy's stubbornness.

Meanwhile the silence between the two friends continued. Ellie was desperately trying to think of something to say to break the awful silence but couldn't come up with anything. Lucy was studiously looking straight ahead totally ignoring Ellie.

"Well, this is it," said Ellie as she stopped the car and turned off the ignition. "How shall we play this if we do get an answer.

Lucy shrugged, completely disinterested.

Ellie finally snapped. "Look, it's obvious you don't want to be here but you are, so the least you could do is talk."

Lucy continued to say nothing. She didn't even acknowledge that Ellie had said anything.

"Come on. I don't know why you came but we can't carry on like this. You can't throw away decades of friendship just like that."

"You've moved on quickly. You have Tammy now. You're new best friend."

"What're you talking about? You're my best friend not her."

"Could have fooled me. You spend a lot of time with her and are involving her in this case."

"Of course, why not? She's at least showing an interest when I can't even get hold of you since you don't take my calls."

"Why should I?"

"I'm your best friend and always will be."

"So what?"

"Surely our friendship should mean more to you than this after so many years."

"I'll live," said Lucy.

Ellie gave up. She could see she wouldn't get any further with Lucy who clearly didn't want to talk.

Getting out of the car she led the way up the path and pressed the doorbell. It could be heard ringing out loud and clear. They were just about to give up when a heavily pregnant lady answered the door. The two women gasped as they recognised Belinda.

"Belinda," said Ellie the first to recover herself. "We're here about Bernard. Is he in. We need to talk to him about Ashley."

Belinda shrugged and said, "He's not in."

"When will he be back?"

"Dunno."

"It sounds as if you don't care either."

"Why should I?"

"You look as if you're expecting his baby."

"His! You've got to be joking."

"Why are you here if it's not his?"

"I rent a room. Ashley introduced us and suggested I move in when my old landlord gave notice."

"Who's the father then?" asked Lucy speaking for the first time. She couldn't help but be interested in the situation that faced them.

"Ashley is of course."

"Did he know?"

Belinda shook her head. "I didn't know myself until after we broke up and then he went to his parents."

"They're dead," said Lucy, now thoroughly involved.

"Oh no I'm sorry to hear that. When did it happen?"

"Years ago."

"But…"

"You mean you didn't know?"

Belinda shook her head. "He was always saying he was going there, even that last time."

Lucy looked at Ellie who raised her eyebrows. Belinda caught the look and said, "You don't believe me but it's true."

"Don't tell me Bernard said he was going to his parents as well," said Lucy a touch sarcastically.

"No he didn't."

"Look can we come in?" said Ellie. "It's easier to talk inside and you'll be better sitting down. Your back must be aching."

Belinda reluctantly stood aside in silence as the two women entered. At least they were being allowed in that was something. Whether they would get the truth was another thing altogether.

"When did you last see Bernard?" asked Lucy.

"A couple of weeks ago. He said he was going on holiday with a friend."

"Have you got a name?"

Belinda shook her head, saying, "It's none of my business I'm just the lodger."

"Didn't you ask when he'd be back?"

Again, Belinda shook her head.

Lucy looked at Ellie, thinking what a waste of time this was. Belinda was obviously setting herself up to be as unhelpful as possible.

"Doesn't it worry you that he might have met the same fate as Ashley?"

"Not really."

"Was he seeing anyone?"

"I really don't know. He never brought anyone home."

"Hmm," said Lucy who was having doubts as to how much Belinda was telling the truth.

"Bernard must have said when he'd be back."

"He might have done," said Belinda evasively.

"Well when was it?"

"This weekend I think."

"So if we come back in a few days he'll be here will he?"

Belinda shrugged. "How do I know. I'm not his secretary. His life is nothing to do with me. I pay rent and that's it. I spend most of the time in my room lying on the bed resting. I get tired quickly now."

Lucy and Ellie were back in the car and sat there, both lost in thought.

Lucy was the first to speak, "You know I become more suspicious of Belinda the more I learn."

"In what way?"

"Well, either she's lying or Ashley lied to her which suggests Ashley didn't trust her for some reason."

"We'll never know the truth unless it's connected to what happened to Ashley and possibly to Bernard."

Lucy shook her head. "It has to be linked somehow or why the lies."

Ellie didn't respond. She was looking at Lucy and seeing the animation on her face. It was possible she had her friend back again.

"In the meantime, what do we do about Bernard. We've learned absolutely zilch."

"I know. It's hard to work out where to go next as that was the only lead we had."

"I suppose all we can do is come back in a few days or a weeks time and see if Bernard is back to speak to him."

"We'll have to get passed Belinda first. She's like a prison guard only with secrets she's not telling."

"Or we turn up at his place of work when he should be back and see what happens."

"We don't need to turn up we could ring again."

"But that way we still won't know the truth especially if we are fobbed off by Helen."

"But we don't know what Bernard looks like so we won't know if we've found him or not."

"Very true I suppose we'll just have to come back and watch the house. He might emerge, especially at the time he would be leaving for work."

"But that will make me late for work."

"Not if I come alone. I'm still not back so I could come."

Ellie smiled inwardly. Lucy was obviously back on board with the mystery and willing to go out and leave Mick for a short while. This visit had obviously done her good and for that Ellie was extremely grateful.

"Anyway, we can't sit here any longer I should get you home to Mick."

"It doesn't matter I could stay out. I left Mick with a cup of tea and a sandwich so he'll be fine for now."

"In that case why don't we go back to mine and see if Tammy is up for a visit. We can discuss it with her then."

Lucy's face took on a closed look and Ellie winced. How could she be so insensitive. Lucy must be jealous of the growing friendship between her and Tammy.

"What is it?" asked Ellie, wanting to bring the problem out into the open and deal with it.

"You seem to have included someone else so we are no longer the duo we were."

Ellie put her hand on Lucy's arm and said, "You're still my best friend. You should be included as well. It's just that Tammy knew Ashley and a bit about the situation. She has been useful in bouncing ideas off. It feels like she has taken over Mick's role. Also don't you think she deserves friends and a chance to be taken outside of her circumstances for a while. Her life must seem like an unbearable existence sometimes."

Lucy looked ashamed of herself. She felt she was being petty and jealous. Of course Ellie was right. Maybe she should give Tammy a chance.

"Ok I'll give her a chance, but I don't have to be happy about it."

"As long as you don't show it to Tammy. She's very sensitive you know and will pick up on it."

"It's all right I'll put my acting skills to the test."

"You better had."

"I'll just ring Mick and make sure he's ok."

Ellie nodded, knowing this was a sensible thought.

"Mick hi…..no, it was a waste of time, except for meeting Belinda there….I'm going back to Ellie's and meeting up with Tammy if that's ok….bye."

Lucy put the phone back in her bag and turned to Ellie with a smile. "He says that's fine."

"Good," said Ellie.

"I think this might mean he's on the mend at last."

"I agree. I'm so glad you've worked it out and are happy to leave him for a bit."

"To be honest I was going stir crazy in the house all the time. I felt like strangling him he was driving me mad."

"I can understand that, but I'm glad you didn't go through with it. I don't want to be visiting you in prison."

Ellie drove along in silence for some time. Each woman being lost in their own thoughts.

"You know something, I've really missed you," said Ellie eventually.

"I've missed you as well. I think I went a bit overboard and got everything out of all proportion."

"Maybe but you're back in the real world again now that's the main thing."

It wasn't long before the two women arrived at Ellie's flat. Instead of going directly upstairs Ellie knocked at Tammy's door. They had to wait a bit for Tammy to make her slow way to let them in.

Tammy's face lit up when she was Ellie and when she saw Lucy the smile encompassed her as well.

Sitting comfortably Ellie recounted what happened at Bernard's.

"I didn't realise Belinda would be there," said Tammy.

"That did leave us a bit speechless to begin with but we recovered ourselves enough to ask for Bernard but he either isn't there or she was lying."

"It's hard to know with her as there seem to be a lot of contradictions with her."

"I'm inclined to think she may be the suspect we are looking for. We don't have enough evidence at the moment but she seems to turn up everywhere. I can't believe it's just coincidence that she turns out to be connected to Bernard as well. She's the one involved with both parties," said Lucy.

"I think you could be right," said Tammy. "By the way how's your husband?"

"He's on the mend. Thank you for asking." Lucy felt ashamed of the way she had felt about Tammy. It seemed Tammy was a genuinely nice person, not someone who wanted to steal her best friend from her.

"Where do we go from here?" asked Tammy.

"We thought we should go back to Bernard's again in a few days and watch for him coming out or going in."

"I'll do that as Ellie will be at work and I'm still taking time off to look after Mick. I'll be back at work soon though I think."

"Your welcome to come round while Ellie is at work and we can talk through what you've discovered."

"Thank you I might take you up on it. I'm not sure it's sensible though because one of us would still have to repeat it to Ellie when she finishes work."

"I see your point. Sorry I didn't think of that. I do get lonely during the day and I   think I was only being selfish."

"Don't worry about it. I don't think you're being selfish and I'd love to pop in to see you whatever the topic of conversation may be."

Tammy smiled gratefully at Lucy, feeling as if she'd found another friend. She could almost be glad things had worked out the way they had because if Ashley hadn't disappeared then she would still have been lonely. These two knew all about her eccentricities and still accepted her as she was. She realised they had suspected her of murder at one point but knew now they believed her and were willing to include her and make her a friend.

Lucy glanced at her watch and said, "Sorry to break up the party but I really should get back to Mick."

Ellie stood up and put her coat on preparing to take her friend home.

"You don't have to really. I could get the bus."

"No, I insist. I brought you here so I can take you home."

"Well ok if you're sure."

The two women bade their goodbyes and promising to drop in again soon leaving Tammy to her own thoughts.

It wasn't long before Ellie and Lucy were home and Lucy invited her friend in for a cup of tea. Ellie wasn't going to refuse as it had been so long and she wanted to see how Mick was doing.

Mick smiled a welcome when he saw Ellie but didn't get up.

"You're looking so much better than when I last saw you," said Ellie.

"I feel it. This enforced rest with Lucy at my beck and call was just what I needed."

"I can see that. You really seem to be coming back to life again."

"I am but I still get tired easily."

"Don't worry I won't out stay my welcome."

"You can stay as long as you like. I'll go upstairs to rest when I need to."

While this exchange had been going on Lucy had been making cups of tea for the three of them. She carried the tray through and set it down on the table.

They sat sipping their tea in a comfortable silence, only broken when Mick asked how they had got on with Bernard. Lucy recounted what had happened.

"Weird, how Belinda turns up there and Bernard disappears," commented Mick.

"That's what we thought," said Ellie. "Tammy said the same thing only she went as far as to suggest Belinda may in fact be the murderer."

"I think I'm inclined to agree with her," said Mick. "Although we can't jump to conclusions when we have no evidence. We still don't know enough to make such an accusation."

"I know. We have to check to see if Bernard really is missing or not. I've agreed to watch the house to see if any male comes and goes for a few days."

"If there is no movement I could ring the company again and try and speak to him. I'll pretend to be an old friend who is trying to get back in touch with him."

"Are you sure that would work?" asked Ellie. "They might be protective of Bernard and not put you through. They might say they'll tell him and give him your number so he can ring if he wants to. Then we'd be no further forward."

"Good thinking I hadn't thought it out very well that's for sure."

"Don't worry about it. All we're doing is throwing ideas out there."

"Could I speak to Helen again to see if I can get more from her?"

"Possibly if we don't get anywhere with waiting for Bernard."

"It might be a good idea anyway because if he has disappeared and we can't watch the house at all hours of the day and night."

"I wonder if Belinda will tell him we called," suggested Lucy.

"I wouldn't have thought so. What would it achieve? He doesn't know anything about us."

"By the way I've just remembered, what do you think of Belinda's pregnancy?" asked Ellie.

"I'm not sure. I'm a bit suspicious to be honest. She obviously is heavily pregnant but I'm not sure she's telling the truth about it being Ashley's."

"I had similar thoughts," said Ellie. "It's hard to know what is truth and what isn't with her as she has obviously lied at some point."

"If we could be absolutely certain when Ashley broke up with her it would help."

"I'll give Tammy a ring and see if she can shed any light on the subject."

Ellie got out her phone and quickly got through to Tammy and posed the question. Ellie nodded and quickly disconnected the call.

"Well that was interesting Tammy hasn't seen Belinda around for approximately a year give or take. She can't be certain of exact timings. She never took that much notice not realising at the time it would be important."

"That makes sense," said Lucy. "It certainly pays to be observant. After this I'll pay more attention to what's going on around me. You never know when you'll need that information."

"I agree, but most of what goes on is just boring every day stuff like Belinda not being around. It's a seemingly minor, innocent detail."

"It's all so complicated," sighed Lucy.

"Yes it is, but we are further forward than we were."

"If we write a list of suspects it could be anyone involved who we currently know about."

"I know but it's better than only knowing Tammy who is definitely not a suspect anymore."

"How can you be so sure?" asked Mick, getting involved for the first time. Until then he'd been happy to listen to what was going on.

"If you'd met her you'd understand."

"Really? She could be faking a lot."

"No she isn't. She's very lonely and desperate for friends as well."

"That could all be an act just to get you off the scent."

"So why would she be so helpful?"

"How do you know she is? Her pretending friendship could be all part of it. If she's friends she keeps you close and finds out how close you are to finding out who was involved. She can also lead you away by dropping red herrings around to take you on a false trail. It might only be a game to her."

Lucy shook her head. "She's genuine. You should have seen her face light up when she saw us today."

"Hmm." Mick still remained highly sceptical and wasn't going to cross anyone off the list until they could be proven innocent. In his mind it was guilt first, innocence second. "I realise I don't know her, she is just a name to me so you could be right but I can also see the other side which could be useful. I would advise caution that's all."

Ellie and Lucy said nothing. They were aware of Mick's views of the criminal justice system. He was worth listening to though as he, as an outsider was able to see what the two women couldn't. If it hadn't been for him they would never have solved their previous case.

Chapter Twenty Two

Lucy yawned. She wasn't used to these early starts after weeks of staying home to look after Mick. This was the second day of looking out for Bernard, or any male who she saw going in and out of the house Belinda was in. So far no sighting of any males. If the same happened tomorrow she would knock on the door and find out if he was home. She had an awful feeling she and Ellie had been right in their suspicions that Bernard might have become the next victim. It was looking as if the deaths were related to the fraud that was being uncovered.

....

"Hi Tammy," said Lucy, answering her phone.

"Hello Lucy, sorry to bother you but I've just spoken to Ashley's company again about Bernard. This time I was sensible and didn't mention I was his girlfriend I just gave my name."

"What happened?" asked Lucy unable to keep the eagerness out of her voice.

"I was wondering if you were free to come round for a cuppa?"

"At the moment I'm sat outside Bernard's house."

"You're wasting your time. I'm afraid you were led on a wild goose chase. Someone doesn't want us to find out anything else."

"I'm intrigued now."

"Come round and I'll tell you what I've found out."

"Ok. I just have to pop home and check on Mick then I'll be on my way. If I can't leave I'll let you know."

Lucy related the conversation to Mick when she got back.

"Are you sure she's telling the truth. There are so many untruths floating around in this case it's hard to know what to believe."

"It could be. At the very least I need to know what she has to say as I'm getting nowhere at the moment. To my way of thinking it's better that knocking on the door and getting Belinda who is known to be a liar."

Mick nodded. "That makes sense to me. Could you make me a cup of tea before you go. I'm feeling a bit weak and tired today."

Lucy immediately looked concerned. "Maybe I shouldn't leave you."

"No I'll be fine with a cuppa and a rest. You go and find out what Tammy has to say. If you stay here we'll both be on tenterhooks wondering what is happening which won't be any good for me."

Lucy agreed. She did as requested and was soon in the car driving to visit Tammy.

When the two women were seated, sipping their tea Tammy got straight to the point. Lucy had discovered this about Tammy early on. She rarely did small talk and could be quite abrupt. Lucy didn't know if this was to conserve precious energy or if it was the way she had always been, not that it mattered it was just an observation on Lucy's part.

"Bernard was at work. I spoke to him briefly. He didn't want to talk for long though, said he was busy. It was difficult not knowing him to know what to ask about. I did find out something interesting though. He doesn't know anyone called Belinda."

Lucy raised her eyebrows. "So Belinda was lying again."

"It would seem so. Also it means that lady you spoke to gave us a completely false address for him."

"Who can be trusted in this web of lies."

"I don't know," said Tammy. "I suppose we can't even be sure Bernard is telling the truth."

"That's a point. Did you find out where he lives."

"I can go further than that and can say that he lives with his partner. Interestingly the address he gave is just a few minutes from the hospital."

"That's handy for Ellie. We could call around there one day after Ellie finishes work."

"I would love to know why Helen lied to us."

"And Belinda as well."

"Yes definitely. Look I must go, Mick isn't feeling too good today so I don't want to leave him for too long."

Tammy looked disappointed for a minute before giving herself a shake and saying goodbye to Lucy. She was rather enjoying the company especially now that she was feeling quite a bit better. She needed to remind herself that she was lucky to have two friends who were happy to spend time with her and include her in what they were doing. But, she also told herself, they had lives of their own and things they needed to get on with. They couldn't spend all their time with her. It sent her mood spiralling downhill as it struck home once again what this dreadful illness had taken from her. She had no family or other friends. Tammy had once been a vivacious young person who loved to party. She was always in the centre of a group of people and liked it that way. It never occurred to her that one day she would be alone and isolated.

Lucy reached home to find Mick eagerly awaiting her return to find out what Tammy had found out.

"That's interesting," he said when Lucy had finished recounting the details of her visit with Tammy. "Someone is definitely busy spinning yarns and we have to work out or guess what is truth and what isn't."

"I know. After what you said earlier I decided to keep an open mind on what Tammy had to say. We have to assume she is telling us the truth though. We'll find out if we go to this second address and find Bernard there alive and well. I'd like to know what he has to say about Ashley's disappearance and the fraud at work."

"You need to question him about Helen and the false address as well. Helen and he probably both know Belinda so how is she involved in this strange affair."

Lucy nodded in agreement. "I'm assuming it must be connected to the fraud and that's what killed Ashley."

"If there even was suspected fraud."

"I hadn't even thought of that but I suppose Helen could have lied considering she did so about the address." Lucy sighed, "This is all becoming too complicated."

"I know, but if you must get involved in murders what do you expect. Of course there will be deceit and red herrings placed in our way. We just have to be cautious and weigh up everything we are told."

"I don't envy the police their job or private investigators for that matter. They get this as a matter of course every day they work."

Mick nodded. "Yet you still want to get yourselves mixed up in murder and mayhem."

"It makes life more interesting certainly."

Mick shook his head. His wife was a mixture of contradictions. On the one hand she was glad she wasn't doing this for a living but she still wanted to be involved. He was just glad she was involving herself again. It had been unhealthy for both of them when her sole focus had been on him. He understood though and had been grateful for her constant presence when he had still felt so ill.

Chapter Twenty Three

"Do you really think we'll get anywhere with Bernard?" asked Ellie as she drove her and Lucy to Bernard's address.

"I really don't know. I don't even know if this is the correct address. We're being given the run around at every turn. Was it even Bernard that Tammy was speaking to when she asked for him?"

"And why would he automatically give his address to someone he doesn't know?"

"You think this is another dead end?"

"Yes I do. We don't know what Bernard looks like so even if a man answers it could be anyone."

Lucy shook her head. "This is almost too much to get around."

"I know. Right this is the address we were given. There's a car shall we knock on the door and take it from there?"

"Let's hope Belinda isn't here as well."

"You've got a point there. Why does she keep turning up?"

"That we'll only know after speaking to Bernard if we're lucky."

Lucy pressed the doorbell and they waited in silence. No one came.

"This is odd," said Lucy. "There is definitely a car here."

"Maybe he doesn't use the car to get to work."

"Surely he would need it as he works over the other side of town."

"He might share driving with a friend like we do."

"I hadn't thought of that."

"Get your brain in gear then."

"You mean I have a brain?"

"Well, a single brain cell, or half a one maybe."

"That's more like it. The problem is I could have left it at home with Mick."

"I suggest you always pack it in your head when you go out, especially if we're investigating. I can't do all the thinking for us."

"Anyway, we're not getting any answer," said Lucy changing the subject back to the whereabouts of Bernard.

"Unless there is someone inside but they're choosing not to answer."

"Come on, whatever the situation we're getting nowhere. Let's go and sit in the car and wait. He may not be home from work yet."

The two women sat in a comfortable silence as they waited and waited. No one came.

"I hope everything's ok in there."

"We'll never know. We can't just gain entrance. We're not the police."

"I'm going to try Tammy to see if she got a phone number for him. That would help."

Lucy sat waiting for Tammy to answer but nothing. Lucy grew concerned for her new friend. She knew Tammy hated missing a call and always answered even if she was feeling particularly unwell.

Giving up she looked at Ellie. "No answer. This is weird."

Ellie's expression took on a sombre one. "I think we should give up on Bernard and check on Tammy."

Lucy nodded in agreement so off they went as fast as they dared considering it was still rush hour and a lot of traffic was about.

"Come on," said Lucy impatiently as they sat at traffic lights.

"You won't get them to change any quicker."

"I know. The worst of it is when they do change we'll probably not get through this time. I'm just worried about Tammy. I've got a bad feeling about this."

"I know what you mean. I'm trying not to think about her though. Bernard and Tammy both disappeared is suspicious."

"Disappeared? How do you know that?" asked Ellie.

"Well they don't appear to be in communication do they?"

"That means nothing at the moment," said Ellie. "Wait and see what happens when we get to Tammy." Truth be told, Ellie was just as worried as Lucy. This whole business was very strange.

It was another twenty minutes before they drew up at Ellie's block of flats. Lucy rushed ahead of Ellie and rung the bell for Tammy. No answer. Ellie tried looking through the window but could see nothing through the net curtain that hung there.

"I've got a key. I'm going in, be ready to call the police if necessary."

Lucy stayed back a bit phone in her hand. Ellie opened the door and calling out to Tammy led the way inside. What she was met with made her gasp. Tammy was leaning against the door of her bedroom with tape over her mouth and around her arms and legs.

Lucy hastily made the call and they waited for the police to arrive. They were instructed not to touch anything so they left Tammy as she was. Fortunately it wasn't long before the car turned up and two police officers entered the flat.

Ellie was pleased to see they were both female, feeling that Tammy would be more comfortable talking to female officers.

"Hello Tammy we're PCs Caldwell and Fitzpatrick."

Tammy said nothing just sat there shivering with reaction to her situation.

"Can you tell me what happened?" asked PC Caldwell gently.

Tammy stayed silent, unable or unwilling to talk. Ellie spoke up, explaining what had been happening recently. The two officers looked grave.

"Is this linked?" asked PC Fitzpatrick.

Tammy gave a slight nod.

"Do you know who did this to you?"

Another brief nod.

"Was it Belinda?" asked Ellie taking a guess.

Again, Tammy nodded.

"So, she is somehow involved then. Just as we thought."

"Who is Belinda?"

Ellie explained in more detail. The two officers became serious as they heard the whole story.

"Did she say anything?" asked PC Caldwell.

Tammy opened her mouth and whispered, "She told me to stay out of her business. It was between her and Ashley. She said if I didn't my friends would be in trouble."

"We can look after ourselves," said Ellie trying to sound strong when her insides were quavering. Lucy said nothing. It was clear what the threat implied and that it was aimed at the two of them.

"Was Bernard mentioned?" asked Lucy after a few minutes silence.

Tammy shook her head.

"We'll pass this on to officers dealing with this case," said PC Caldwell. "It's with CID now."

"Are you sure you're ok. We can call an ambulance."

Tammy shook her head. No way did she want them to turn up. Not only would she have to go into detail about what had happened but she would have to deal with their attitude towards ME which was never great. She already felt traumatised from what Belinda had put her through. She didn't want to discuss it with the police, it would only lead to more trouble.

Tammy breathed a huge sigh of relief when the police left her flat. It wasn't over, she realised, knowing the detectives dealing with the case would be in touch but she had got assurances it wouldn't be that day.

"What happened?" asked Ellie when they were all sitting sipping cups of tea which she had made as soon as the police left.

"Belinda knocked at the door and when I opened it she barged right in. I asked what she wanted and she said it was a message for us to keep out of her business. She'd warned me once and now she was going to show me she meant it. If we continued she would do more than this. She hinted there would be trouble for you as well."

"I wonder how she is mixed up in it all," said Lucy. "She is so pregnant…"

"There was no sign of pregnancy when she was here," said Tammy. "I'd forgotten that you'd said she was when you saw her at that house."

"What's going on then? This is very strange. Why pretend?"

"Maybe she thought she would get away with anything if she were pregnant."

"Maybe…I'm not convinced though," said Ellie. "We thought it strange that it could be Ashley's anyway the dates didn't quite add up."

"I hope Bernard is ok. It seems possible he could have met the same fate as Ashley," said Lucy.

"If it were safe to do so I would go back round to where we met Belinda and find out what she has to say for herself. In my mind it seems possible that she is the murderer of Ashley and the one behind all of this."

"I wonder what Mick would come up with," said Lucy. "I think we need a good old chat and see where we go from here."

"I agree," said Ellie. "As long as Mick is up to discussing this."

"He should be."

"Great, why don't we head there now and let Tammy rest."

"Are you all right with that?" asked Lucy, concerned at the colour of Tammy's face.

Tammy shook her head. She was still feeling very shaken up with what had happened and didn't feel at all safe at being left on her own.

"Would you rather I stayed with you?" asked Ellie.

Tammy nodded gratefully.

"Ok. I'll stay. Are you all right with that Lucy?"

Lucy nodded. "I'll see what Mick has to say then I'll ring you and let you know. Obviously if he has questions I can't answer I'll ring as well."

Lucy said goodbye to the two women and left. She was a bit reluctant as Tammy wasn't looking at all well and she wasn't sure Ellie would be able to manage on her own if anything were to happen.

"Why don't I help you to bed?" said Ellie when Lucy had shut the door behind her.

"I don't want to. I'm afraid if I go to sleep I'll have awful nightmares."

"It must have really frightened you when Belinda burst in."

"It did. More than you'll ever know. She threatened Mick if we continued investigating but I didn't want to say that in front of Lucy."

"I can understand that. It means that she must have been following us or at least asking questions if she knew about Mick."

Tammy nodded. "I didn't get the chance to ask how she knew as she straight away put tape over my mouth to keep me quiet."

"I'm just glad I had a key to get in or you would have been left like this longer."

"It was quite long enough as it was," said Tammy.

"I'm sure it must have felt like forever."

"Belinda was here ages – or so it seemed."

"Did she do or say anything else which might help us?"

"She had a knife which she held at my throat." Tammy started shaking violently as this came back into her mind.

Ellie didn't know what to say. It was clear Tammy was very frightened but what could she do? The police should have been told this when they were here so more urgent action could be taken. Also it could alert them that Belinda could be dangerous.

"I know what you're thinking. I couldn't tell the police as it would only made things worse."

"They need to know though so they can deal with the situation appropriately."

"They wouldn't believe me."

"Why not? It's obvious something serious had taken place because you were tied up."

"Belinda said she would deny all knowledge and make out it was me who threatened her. The police would believe her especially if she were looking pregnant again."

"It would be easy to prove she wasn't though."

"How? The police wouldn't be able to take risks like that in case it was real. It would only be our word against hers."

"Let's see what Mick and Lucy can come up with before we panic. I think we need to tell them all this..." She stopped as Tammy shook her head. "...I know you don't want to but they can deal with things more appropriately if they know everything."

Very reluctantly Tammy agreed with a nod of her head. Ellie picked up her phone and keyed in Lucy's number. On hearing Lucy's voice Ellie quickly updated her on what Tammy had said.

"Right....ok...I'll let Mick know and see what he says. I hadn't had a chance to say anything so I'll add that into the story."

"That sounds interesting," said Mick when Lucy put the phone down.

"You'll not believe what has been going on."

"Try me."

Lucy quickly related all they had discovered adding in what Ellie had just told her.

"This is dangerous. I'm not sure I like you getting involved anymore," said Mick.

"It's no worse than when we were investigating Phyllis's death. If anything we're safer with this because we haven't met all those that play a part in it."

"I think you have, except for Bernard maybe."

"He might not even be alive."

"True."

"Do you think you know who did it then?"

"I still have my doubts over Tammy."

"What, even though she was tied up and given a warning?"

"It could be bogus to make you think she's innocent and to stop looking into it yourselves."

"I don't see that. I'm sure she's innocent."

"She maybe but we only have her word for everything."

"She got us the address for Bernard remember."

"Only if it was the true address. It could be false."

"Why? What would be her motive."

"Now that I don't know."

Lucy shook her head. "I think we'll have to agree to disagree as I'm one hundred percent sure she's innocent."

"That's up to you of course. You know her better than I do, having never met her."

"What do we do about Bernard?"

"My thought is to try again at a different time. See if you can see in through windows again and try doors to see if they're open."

"You think we should go inside?"

"If you can it would be good. See what you can find."

Lucy nodded and decided to phone Ellie with a summary of the conversation. Ellie was surprised Mick still thought Tammy was involved but was happy to go with his idea of getting into Bernard's house.

Chapter Twenty Four

"Well, here goes," said Ellie.

"You sound hesitant," replied Lucy.

"Not really, just wary of what might be waiting for us."

"No one knows what we're doing."

"Tammy does."

"Now you're buying into Mick's theory of Tammy's guilt."

"Not really but it helps to be prepared."

"You're getting me scared now."

"Sorry, that wasn't my intention."

After this exchange Ellie finally took the decision to ring the bell. Again, there was no answer in spite of the car being in the drive.

"Oh well here goes," said Lucy as she tried the door and nearby windows.

They managed to open the side gate and walked through to what looked like a massive garden. It was well taken care of from a quick glance. There were flowers and what looked like vegetables growing opposite the flowers. It was immaculate.

"This must take time looking after it."

"It does," said a male voice behind them.

The two friends jumped, completely startled.

"Who are you?" asked Ellie, recovering herself quickly.

"Shouldn't I be asking you that," said the man.

From a quick observation he was tall and good looking, at least to Ellie. He wore glasses and was clean shaven. He looked to be in his thirties.

"We're Ellie and Lucy," said Ellie. "You must be Bernard."

A brief nod confirmed this to be true.

"We did try ringing the doorbell but when we got no answer we came to have a look around. We were worried about your wellbeing."

"Well as you can see I'm fine. What do you want with me? By the way the doorbell doesn't work properly."

Ellie and Lucy glanced at each other. Both had been certain they'd heard it give a slight ring.

"We wanted to ask you some questions about Ashley," said Ellie, taking the lead. Lucy was content to let her. She wanted to listen as something seemed off but she wasn't sure what it was.

"When was the last time you saw Ashley? How was he? Why did he leave his job?"

"Slow down I can't answer them all at once if you keep flying questions my way. Ashley was a close friend of mine. No, actually he was more than a close friend. We were sort of seeing each other."

"Sort of?" queried Lucy, getting in on the conversation.

Bernard nodded. "Ashley wasn't keen on us seeing each other openly. He'd only recently broken up with his girlfriend you see."

"Was that Belinda by any chance?"

Bernard nodded again.

"He discovered there was fraud being committed at work which lost him his job and probably his life."

"Do you know who it was?"

Bernard shook his head. "He never confided in me."

"You were so close you were actually seeing each other but he didn't tell you who was committing a crime."

"He wanted to protect me from harm. He said it was for the best if I didn't know."

"Why should he assume it could be dangerous?"

"He'd been threatened to keep quiet and say nothing."

"Even when his body was found you didn't come forward."

"I didn't think I had any evidence as to what took place."

"But you knew of a possible motive for his death which should have been passed on to the police."

"I couldn't be sure that's why he was killed or any idea who may have done it."

Ellie nodded in agreement, but Lucy could tell Ellie wasn't totally with it. Was it possible she knew who was responsible?

"Ok we'll leave you to it," said Ellie abruptly and dragging Lucy behind her they hastily left Bernard alone.

"What was all that about?" asked Lucy.

"Let's get out of here then I'll tell you."

Lucy had to be satisfied with that. She knew Ellie would tell her what was happening when she was ready and not before. In fact it wasn't until they got back to Lucy's that they realised what a negative impact it would have if Ellie were to speak.

"You think it was Bernard don't you?" queried Lucy.

Ellie nodded, "But keep it to yourself."

They jumped in and Bernard waved them off. When they were on their way Lucy tried again to get information out of Ellie, to no avail.

"I want us to get back home before we talk. I need some thinking time."

Lucy stayed quiet and said nothing. She knew Ellie well enough to know if she didn't want to say anything then she wouldn't until she was ready. True to her word Ellie kept quiet, lost in thought. She was sure there were gaps in the story as she was working it out in her mind.

When they got back to Lucy's Ellie finally spoke, "Is Mick well enough to come to see Tammy? I want to let Tammy know at the same time."

"You're really certain aren't you?"

Ellie nodded. "I'm sure Bernard is the one we are looking for."

"How do you know that? He seemed all right to me."

"He said hardly anything though."

"Maybe, but do you blame him after the way we appeared and the things we said."

"I suppose not but I still think it was him and I don't want to leave anyone out of the story and that includes Tammy. Besides if I'm right she or Mick could be in danger now the truth is coming out."

"Surely Bernard doesn't know you suspect him."

"Probably not but I'm not taking any chances. He's a criminal, committing fraud and then murder."

"Was that his motive for killing Ashley then?"

"I think so although without hearing it from him I can't be totally sure."

"Why do you think it's him? He didn't say anything."

"He did actually. Remember he said he didn't know who was committing fraud."

"Yeah. So what?"

"Well think back to Helen who said Bernard knew about it."

"That could just mean Helen was lying as she later lied about his address. If anything it's most likely to be Helen."

"How do you know Bernard is telling the truth?"

"It fits in with what Tammy told us."

"You're not going to convince me otherwise. Bernard is the killer. I think he knew we were there all along. We heard the doorbell ring but Bernard didn't because it's not working. That's a lie we can prove."

"Ok so he lied about that. Belinda and Helen have also lied to us about more serious things."

They soon arrived back at Lucy's. Ellie waited in the car while Lucy went in to see if Mick was up to a trip to Tammy's. They took their time and Ellie started getting impatient. She was so certain she knew what was going on and wanted to end it as soon as possible. Also it would hopefully get Mick off the subject of Tammy as killer.

Ellie happened to glance up into the rear view mirror and noticed a car sat a short way behind. If she was right it was following them. She couldn't be sure how she knew this she just did. She beeped the horn hoping to hurry her friends up. She was getting the creeps as well as frightened. She wanted to get moving to see what happened with the car.

Eventually Lucy and Mick emerged and got in the car.

"What was the beeping about?" asked Lucy. "I was helping Mick get ready. He was keen to come when I explained the situation."

"I think we're being followed," said Ellie as she rapidly pulled out and started the drive to Tammy's.

Lucy looked round but couldn't see anything. "Are you sure? Maybe you're just getting jumpy. I can't see anyone following."

"Well I suppose it could be just another parked car." Ellie remained unconvinced, but didn't want to frighten her friends too much unless she had to. Mick was still quite fragile, she needed to remember that.

As they continued on their way Ellie noticed the same car some distance behind them. She was right. They were being followed. Who was it though? She was too far ahead to see who was driving, although she was certain it would be someone they knew and probably was the murderer. Did this mean they were getting close? There had been no threat before and now Tammy tied up and they were being followed. It couldn't be any coincidence.

"Now what are they doing?"

"Who?" asked Lucy.

"The car behind that's been following us."

Lucy looked behind and saw the car speeding up. "They're getting closer, can't you go any faster?"

"Not safely. I'm already over the speed limit. I don't want points on my licence thank you."

The car was gaining on them. Lucy started to tense up. This shouldn't be happening and what would it do to Mick on the one occasion he was leaving the house. She glanced at Mick who was sat in the back. He was looking pale and worried.

"Are you all right darling?"

"I'm not sure," he replied. "Chest getting tight."

"Maybe we should detour to the hospital," said Lucy. "We can always call the police from there."

"I don't think we'll have a chance. He's gaining on us."

At that moment they felt a bang as the car behind went into them.

"Is everyone ok?" asked Ellie.

Lucy and Mick shook their heads. Lucy felt as if she'd jarred her neck a bit and Mick was now getting pain in his chest again.

"We need to stop," said Lucy.

"I think we're safer if we carry on," said Ellie. "We can call the police and ambulance from Tammy's. Hopefully we'll be safe then. Can you see who's in the car?"

Lucy strained trying to see who it could be but couldn't see anything. Instead she winced at the pain in her neck at the movement.

Mick turned and looked saying, "It's a man."

"It must be Bernard then. Exactly as I thought," said Ellie with a note of triumph in her voice.

Lucy leaned her aching head back against the seat rest and closed her eyes. She was starting to feel quite sick.

"Are you all right?" asked Ellie with a sideways glance at her friend.

Lucy shook her head and winced at the pain it set off.

"We'll soon be at Tammy's then we'll be safe to get help."

"I don't think we should carry on," said Mick.

"If we stop we're at risk of being rammed harder or goodness knows what happening."

Mick didn't respond, seeing the truth in Ellie's statement.

The drive continued but it seemed like the longest journey they had ever made. Every few minutes there was another bump as the car behind rammed them.

Lucy, by now, was beyond speech. She had her eyes shut hoping she wouldn't be sick in the car, but her head and neck were aching badly. The jolting movement every time the other car went into them made the pain worse. It was with much relief when they drove into the car park belonging to the flats. Ellie stopped but made no attempt to get out, instead she made the emergency call and then phoned Tammy to let her know what was happening and where they were.

Tammy getting the message looked out of the window and saw her friend's car sitting there. She wondered if she could possibly make it if she tried walking to them. It would be the furthest she had walked for several years. She didn't relish the pain it would cause but at the same time wanted to be with them. She hated being in this dilemma. Anyone else would be able to go out and help but she had to weigh up the pros and cons first. ME, how she hated it. It had stolen her life and she saw no prospect of it ever ending. Grabbing her stick she tried to make it outside. She took it slowly, stopping every few steps for a rest. So slow was she that the police had already arrived by the time she reached the car.

Ellie quickly explained to PC Caldwell what had happened.

"You seem to be attracting trouble," said the officer with a tone of disapproval. "The same address in such a short space of time. Is an ambulance coming or do we need to call one."

"It's on its way," said Ellie. She was starting to feel as if what had happened was all her fault. There was certainly no sympathy coming from the officers.

"Where is this car that was supposedly following you?" asked PC Fitzpatrick.

"I don't know," said Ellie in a whisper.

"Without any evidence to the contrary maybe it was your dangerous driving that caused the damage. You could be making up about the other car to get out of trouble when you realised your friends were hurt."

"That isn't it at all."

"Did you see this other car?" asked PC Caldwell of Tammy when she finally reached her friends.

Tammy reluctantly shook her head. She wished she could lie but that would only cause more trouble as she couldn't give any information about the other car. She was sure Ellie was telling the truth but had no idea what to say.

The two officers inspected the damage to the car and became even more suspicious when all they saw was a slight dent in the bumper and a broken light. They looked at each other before moving to the drivers side again.

"Out you get," said PC Caldwell to Ellie. "We're going to have to breathalyse you."

"But I don't drink at this time of day and certainly not when driving." Ellie was feeling deeply offended by what was happening.

"We can't take your word for that I'm afraid," said PC Fitzpatrick rather severely.

Ellie got out of the car with a heavy sigh.

"If you don't cooperate we'll have to arrest you anyway and take you to the station," said PC Caldwell.

Ellie felt close to tears. She'd never been in trouble with the police but she was the one being treated like a criminal. Breathing into their machine she waited to be given the all clear.

"Let's see your documents to make sure you have a legal right to drive this car."

This was too much for Tammy who couldn't help butting in. "Why can't you take her word for it. Isn't it obvious what happened and that she's telling you the truth."

"Not really. You could have tied yourself up the other day with someone to help you."

Tammy couldn't believe what she was hearing. The officers really seemed to have it in for them but the question was why.

"Why don't you believe us?" asked Tammy, feeling brave enough to challenge this attitude.

"You lied about being tied up so why should we believe anything else you or your friends say."

Tammy was dumbstruck and stared open mouthed at what she was hearing.

"By rights we should arrest the lot of you for wasting police time."

"How can you say that?"

"Easily. We had an interesting chat with Belinda who told us everything. It seems your friend Ashley and you were involved in defrauding the company. Apparently it was your idea. We had to call an ambulance for Belinda whose pregnancy was at risk because of the stress of our questions."

"What pregnancy? She was fine when she was threatening me. She didn't even look overweight."

"We know a pregnant woman when we see one and she most definitely was. She was taking off to the hospital as a precaution. Fortunately for you the baby is ok."

Tammy and Ellie glanced at each other. It was clear to them that they wouldn't get any help from the police. They believed everything Belinda said. She must be a very convincing actress.

It was at this point that the ambulance turned up.

One of the paramedics went to Lucy who was still sat in the car with her eyes shut. She was beyond moving at that time. Even answering questions was too much. Ellie told them the story of the car, ignoring the snort of disapproval from one of the police officers.

"This injury would certainly be consistent with what you say," said the paramedic.

"Are you telling me that it happened as they say it did?" asked PC Caldwell, still with that incredulous tone.

The paramedic nodded. "I can't see any other cause of such an injury."

The other paramedic was in the back with a now grey faced Mick. "We need to get this one to hospital as soon as possible."

Calling for another ambulance the paramedic with Lucy stood up and went to assist with Mick. The police stood around unsure what their next move should be. They had been so certain of the cause of events that now everything was put in doubt. PC Caldwell didn't want to believe Ellie but now it seemed as if evidence was pointing to it being the truth. This led to the thought that maybe Tammy's version of events might be correct as well. In which case it was Belinda who had been spinning them a yarn and had faked pregnancy to stay out of trouble.

PC Caldwell put a call out on her radio with the details of the other car that Ellie had noticed. Ellie was glad her powers of observation were so good. It enabled her to give the information needed and to be accurate.

PC Caldwell came off her radio and spoke to Ellie, "Do you know a Phillip Granger?"

Ellie shook her head.

"He's not involved in this investigation of yours?"

"Not at all."

PC Caldwell said, "That's who the car is registered to."

Ellie shrugged her shoulders, having not heard the name mentioned at all.

At that moment PC Caldwell had a call through. She withdrew slightly to take the call in confidence. She looked across at Ellie as she listened.

Ellie didn't know how to interpret the look. It could be good or bad news.

PC Caldwell approached her when she finished the call and said, "The car has been stopped. It has some damage to the front which would be consistent with going into the back of you. The driver of the car is one Bernard Granger. It seems he's the brother of this Philip who owns the car."

"Bernard? Yes, we spoke to him at his house before leaving to come here."

"We have to interview him of course, but first I need to take a statement from you if that's all right."

Ellie nodded. She just wanted to get it over and done with. She hoped this case was now coming to an end. She repeated everything to PC Caldwell right from the start of this with the blood in the bath. She finished by mentioning her suspicions that Bernard might be the killer of Ashley.

"Thank you," said the officer. "Hopefully we'll have everything we need to wrap the case up. We're very grateful for all you've done to help solve it although we don't usually encourage members of the public to investigate cases, but this time it seems to have paid off. You must be careful, by getting involved in serious crimes you are putting yourself and your friends at risk."

Ellie nodded, looking sombre. PC Caldwell feeling she had said enough decided to leave the scene. There was nothing more to be done here. She knew where to find Ellie if she needed more information.

Tammy, who had been standing to the side while all this had been going on, said, "Why don't you come into mine for a cup of tea. You look as if you could do with something hot and sweet."

"I want to go to the hospital with my friends. I need to know they are both all right."

Tammy nodded, feeling disappointed but understood.

"Look I'll come in for a bit when I get back."

Tammy brightened up at this. "Ok see you later."

Ellie got in her car and followed the ambulance to the hospital. She hurried into A and E after parking the car and asked for her friends at reception. She was directed to a waiting area where she took a seat. She had to wait until a doctor came out and spoke to her.

Lucy was suffering from whiplash and shock. She just needed to rest. There was more concern over Mick but he was being seen and was once again hooked up to monitors which were beeping every few seconds.

"What happened?" whispered Lucy.

"It seems it was Bernard who was following us and trying to cause us to have a serious accident."

"So you were right then."

"It looks like it but don't know anything for sure. I don't know if we ever will know the full story as the police don't seem all that impressed with us."

"But we solved the case for them."

"That's true but I still got a lecture on how dangerous it can be investigating cases on our own."

"I can see their point I suppose. It doesn't look good for them either if members of the public take to doing their job for them."

"That's very true. Are you free to go?"

"Yes I think so. I'm waiting to see about Mick though. You go if you want to get back."

"No it's ok, I'll wait. Tammy will only want to know how you both are so I'd better wait and see what's happening."

Lucy nodded as the two women sat together waiting anxiously for news on Mick.

"What are you two sat here for?" asked Mick, approaching them.

"What are you doing here?" asked Ellie.

"I've been given the all clear and an earlier appointment with the consultant."

"You were all hooked up to machines."

"I know but everything was fine. I just need to rest and take it easy for a few days."

"Ok the car's outside I'll drive you home and then go on to see Tammy."

"We might as well all go to Tammy and discuss things."

"Are you sure?" asked Lucy. "You are supposed to be taking it easy you just said so yourself."

"I feel I owe her an apology," said Mick.

"I don't think that's a good idea as she doesn't know you had her as the leading suspect."

"I know but I'd like to meet her all the same."

"Well ok if you're sure I suppose I can take us all back to hers."

It wasn't long before they were piling into Tammy's small sitting room and talking all at once.

"Please can we talk one at a time," said Tammy. "It's exhausting trying to listen to you altogether."

"Sorry," said Ellie.

They each recounted what they knew of the situation as Tammy listened.

"We still don't know how Belinda fits into all of this. And what about Helen she also lied to us about the information she was feeding us."

"Maybe they don't."

It was at that moment the doorbell rang. Tammy rose slowly to her feet and went to answer it.

"What do you want?" asked Tammy.

Ellie, hearing the tone of voice realised something was wrong went to the door to be confronted by Belinda. An angry looking Belinda.

"It's your fault. My brother has been arrested because of you lot. Why did you have to stick your nose in where it wasn't wanted."

"Sorry? Who's your brother?" asked Tammy.

"Bernard," responded Belinda.

"Oh that makes sense now," said Ellie.

"It does. I'm glad you think so. He'll never survive in prison. You've effectively killed him."

"He shouldn't have killed Ashley then."

"He was forced into it. If Ashley had kept his nose out of our business he would still be alive."

"So you both committing fraud then," stated Lucy.

"I'm saying nothing in response to that."

"You don't need to, you've all but admitted it. Plus there is your attack and threats made to Tammy which put you nicely in the frame."

Belinda put her hand in her bag and pulled out a gun which she pointed at all of those present. "Now who's in control. I warned you what would happen. I couldn't have timed it better. You're all together. Perfect."

"You're already in enough trouble why make it worse by killing us?"

"I've got nothing to lose. With you lot out of the way there will be no one to accuse us of anything. We'll go free."

"Helen knows."

"She knows nothing except what we've been feeding her. We give her inaccurate information which she has been feeding you with."

Tammy put her hand out to lean against the wall to stop herself from falling. What Belinda didn't know was that there was an alarm there she could press if she needed help. It was in an ideal position for Tammy to lean her bottom against it and set it off. She felt herself relax, help would soon be there and Belinda would be arrested. Hopefully she had done it in time to save herself and her friends from being shot. All she could hope was that it wouldn't cause Mick another heart scare.

It was a short while later that the police car drove up to a halt outside the flats. The police approached and finding the doors open went inside to see Belinda waving her gun around. Fortunately it didn't look as if there were any casualties at that moment. This would take careful handling though.

"Ok put the gun down. You're surrounded," said the first officer to enter.

The other officer taking in the situation at a glance withdrew and called for back up because a suspect was armed.

Belinda started firing the gun wildly around, knowing it was all over for her. The bullets were hitting the walls as she had completely lost control and was aiming all over the place. A relief to everyone else in the room.

"That's enough," said the officer. "You don't really want anyone to get hurt."

"I wouldn't have a gun if I didn't want to shoot anyone. Of course I want to hurt people. I want them all dead and that includes you." Once again she took aim and fired hitting the officer square in the chest. He fell back, hand clutching where the bullet went in. Blood was squirting everywhere. It was obvious he wasn't going to survive. It was just minutes before his eyes glazed over and stared unseeing up at the ceiling.

"Who wants to be next?" asked Belinda, who had now gained control of the gun.

There was no response from anyone.

"Why don't you give yourself up. There are more officers on the way," said the other officer entering the room again.

"You want to be next? Ok take this then." Once again Belinda fired but this time nothing happened.

She tried again and again but nothing. She looked in desperation at the gun to see what was wrong. She knew there were still bullets in it so it must have jammed in someway. Seeing nothing for it she put it on the ground and the officer went over and quickly handcuffed her. The scene was secure when back up arrived minutes later. The only casualty was the police officer. None of the friends had been injured and were fine if shocked by the turn of events.

Ellie and Lucy looked at each other satisfied. They had successfully solved another case and gained a new friend at the same time. Tammy looked around happily at her newfound friends, knowing she need never be lonely again.

9 781916 083257